ABEL SANCHEZ

MIGUEL de UNAMUNO

ABEL SANCHEZ AND OTHER STORIES

Translated by Anthony Kerrigan

Introduction by
Mario J. Valdez
University of Toronto

Gateway Editions

Library of Congress Cataloging-in-Publication Data
Unamuno, Miguel de. 1864-1936.
[Novels. English. Selections]
Abel Sanchez and other stories / Miguel de Unamuno : introduction by Mario Valdes.
p. cm.
Contents: Abel Sanchez–The madness of doctor Montarco-San Manuel Bueno, Martyr.
ISBN 0-89526-707-1 (alk. paper)
1. Unamuno, Miguel de, 1864-1936-Translations into English.
I. Title.
PQ9639.N3A28 1996
868'.6209–DC20 96-20645
CIP

Published in the United States by
Gateway Editions
An imprint of Regnery Publishing
A Division of Salem Media Group
300 New Jersey Avenue NW
Washington, DC 20001
www.Regnery.com

Manufactured in the United States of America
2020 Printing

Distributed to the trade by
Perseus Distribution
250 West 57th Street
New York, NY 10107

CONTENTS

Introduction by Mario J. Valdes vii

Abel Sanchez 3

The Madness of Doctor Montarco 179

San Manuel Bueno, Martyr 207

INTRODUCTION

Spain is a nation of opposites that enlarge and expand beyond ordinary contradictions; these polarities are in evidence in Spain's geography, linguistic diversity, cultural makeup, history, politics, and, of course, its art. This is the country of Luis Buñuel, Pablo Casals, Pablo Picasso, Joan Miró, Salvador Dali, and Federico García Lorca—all artists of this century whose work reflects the intimate and public tensions of a society forever engaged in a shifting dialectic of polarities. Of all the great artists and thinkers of Spain's twentieth century no one looms so large and so central to an understanding of present-day Spain as Miguel de Unamuno (1864–1936). To understand Unamuno's work is to understand Spain, and to understand Spain is to understand Unamuno.

This book, a kind of essential Unamuno reader, contains three narratives by Unamuno: "The Madness of Doctor Montarco," a short story written and published in 1904; *Abel Sánchez,* a novel written and published in 1917; and *San Manuel Bueno, Martyr,* written in 1930 and published in book form in 1933. These three dates mark equidistant points in Unamuno's writing career. In 1904 he was forty years old and at the beginning of his career as an author, still very much the iconoclastic rebel demanding the regeneration of Spain after the debacle of the Spanish-American war of 1898. By 1917 Unamuno was at his intellectual summit. He had recently published his major philosophical essay, "The Tragic Sense of Life" (1913), and his modernist masterpiece, the novel *Niebla/Mist* (1914). He, together with José Ortega y Gasset, was the intellectual power of Spain. While Ortega y Gasset sought to make Spain an intellectual partner in Europe, Unamuno passionately threw himself into the task of challenging the way Spaniards considered themselves as a nation. Unamuno set about provoking Spaniards of all walks of life to think for themselves and to reject dogmatic thinking. The year 1930 was the time of the last great effort by the old warrior; he had recently returned in triumph from exile in France amidst great expectations for political freedom with the beginning of the Second Spanish Republic (1931–1936).

San Manuel was first published in 1931, and in book form in 1933, at a time of turmoil and the cataclysmic political extremism that in only three years would result in the tragic sea of blood of the Spanish Civil War (1936–1939). Unamuno died on December 31, 1936, defiant, independent, and rebellious to the end. He lived seventy-two years, half in the nineteenth century and half in the twentieth, and he wrote the way he lived—with intensity and passion, the unrivaled defender of the rights of the individual and the community of individuals against the arbitrary rule of the state. In many ways his political views were half a century ahead of his time; he rejected all political systems that suppress individual rights, whether these are invoked in the name of god, nation, or political party. To Unamuno all dogmatism is the same: the effective denial of the individual's right to form a community of individuals.

Perhaps the most valuable introduction I can give the general reader is to contextualize the three narratives, both historically and intellectually. "The Madness of Doctor Montarco" was published in a popular monthly magazine, *La España moderna,* and has been reprinted in Spanish only in the complete works of Unamuno. Its inclusion in this volume was the decision of the late Anthony Kerrigan, translator and editor, who first put together this book in 1956. A number of specific historical and biographical factors are interwoven by Unamuno in this story. The most obvious is the allusion to the public reception of Unamuno's radically modernist parody of sociology in *Amor y pedagogía* (Love and Pedagogy; 1902) as a work that was purported to be inappropriate for a university professor. We can also discern a number of Unamuno's most seminal ideas about life and society. He often caused consternation when he wrote that the instinct that most impels humans to act is not self-preservation as the social Darwinists would have but rather the instinct of wanting more, the appetite to be god—that is, to continue to be the person one is but, also, to encompass and assimilate what one wants from the other. In this story the protagonist remarks that reason and the effective use of reason are not ends in themselves but tools and weapons to be used in the struggle for life as the individual's personal domain. The narrator makes the observation, often made by Unamuno in his essays, that reason is a conservative force dedicated to the preservation of the established order that protects life as it is known at the time and will tolerate challenges only to the extent that they do not threaten this order. The often repeated assertion was that reason must be used in the service of passion or, as Goya would have it, when reason dreams it produces monsters. Unamuno's strong characters, like Pachico of *Peace in*

War or Gertrudis of *La tía Tula* (Aunt Tula), are wide awake and know what they want to accomplish, and they use their rational powers of analysis to achieve it. The moral philosophy of Unamuno rested on the mutual respect of individuals, each with his or her desire to be, and whose differences would be adjudicated by the use of reason.

Doctor Montarco's reading habits are also Unamuno's, who read *Don Quixote* as a philosophical text and who was very well informed on British and German science. Quite clearly, the unconventional doctor also shared with Unamuno his complete rejection of the generic categories of essay, prose fiction, drama, and poetry; Unamuno's concern as a reader of others and as a writer was with the author's situation within the text. The organization of a text is to Unamuno a construction of fundamental polarities which are more or less hidden, more or less revealed by the specific linguistic elements used. Style to Unamuno is not only self-expression but a translucent presentation of the inherent conflict in the author's point of view. Consequently, the more the written words tend to obscure the author's inner conflict, the less it is a matter of style and the more it becomes gesturing.

And thus it is in this short story. On the surface the conflict of the good doctor appears to be trivial: he wants to have a private life as a writer of creative prose as well as a professional life as a doctor devoted to general practice in provincial Spain. The reader should recognize immediately that this situation is a clear parallel to that of Unamuno himself, who by 1904 was professor of Greek and Latin at the University of Salamanca and also author of *Amor y pedagogía,* one of the most outlandish parodies of intellectual life in Spain. But even a surface probe into the story of Doctor Montarco reveals a much deeper conflict: a virtual existential polemic between the person *others* think we are and, therefore, the one we try to act out, like a dramatic role, and the person *we* think we are or would like to be. The problem is that these personae are not fixed but rather are embarked on a conflictive process of development. The public persona is constantly threatening to take over the identity of the private persona and, on the other side, the private persona despises the hypocrisy of the public persona and tends to blame others for forcing the self to play this part.

In this story, it is the narrator who observes the public persona and, through his friendship, gains access to glimpses of the private persona. As the story begins we are informed that this is a new beginning for the doctor, who was forced to leave his hometown and start anew in the present place of practice. The balance between the public and private personae appears to be working; however, the narrator foreshadows the conflictive situation which lies ahead by informing us that Doctor Montarco confessed to him that there are gestures which are natural enough at first but later become artificial after they have been repeatedly praised. But there are also other gestures which we have acquired by imitation and hard work that end up by becoming completely natural to us. The slippage between the two is constant as long as the public and private faces are more or less equal. The war begins when one side is thrown off balance because of external pressure. Two days after publishing a story halfway between fantasy and humor, Montarco is deeply upset. The townspeople, it seems, look askance at a doctor who is all seriousness in his practice of medicine and, nevertheless, is capable of writing farce. Poor Doctor Montarco loses his practice and is sent to an insane asylum under the care of a former fellow medical student, Dr. Atienza, and it is here that the story takes its last and most unusual turn. The real transgression of Doctor Montarco was not breaking some code of propriety for a doctor, but rather attempting to get people to think for themselves, to reconsider and redescribe the world they have accepted so uncritically.

Unamuno's *Abel Sánchez* can be called psychoanalytic fiction, for it clearly delves into the psychosis of pathological envy by means of a narrative alternating between a third-person and a first-person narrator. Unamuno was not only interested in the schizoid condition in individuals but also considered these symptoms at the level of communities.

In the novel, Abel Sánchez, is the object of pathological envy on the part of his lifelong friend and companion, Joaquín Monegro, who ironically and symbolically is the protagonist in the story that has his friend's name as its title. Abel is congenial and well liked by all; Joaquín is willful, aggressive, and extremely competitive, not unlike the young Unamuno. From the outside—that is, the perspective of the third-person narrator—the reader's sympathy is with Abel. Joaquín is too intense, too overbearing, and the reader, like the characters in the novel, tires of this constant harangue from this problematic character. Yet we also have the selected first-person entries from Joaquín's diary, which provide insight into a wounded and painfully obsessed victim of a psychosis of severe insecurity.

In Joaquín's first entry into his diary, he begins to portray himself as the reverse image of his friend, in spite of the fact that they are not opposites but merely different. Yet it is Joaquín who constructs the oppositional character traits of the two: Abel is the congenial one, and Joaquín, the antipathetic one, without either one knowing why this is so. Joaquín has been left alone. Ever since childhood his friends have left him to himself.

Joaquín's obsessive envy of Abel is nurtured and matures. When Abel informs him that he will marry Helena, the young woman the two friends have courted, Joaquín writes in his diary that he felt as if his soul had frozen, the icy cold pressed upon his emotions as "if flames of ice were suffocating me." Joaquín nurtures a hatred for Helena and even more for Abel.

Years later the British psychiatrist R. D. Laing was to write a description of frantic envy that could have been a description of Joaquín Monegro (although it is doubtful whether Laing knew of *Abel Sánchez* since his book, *The Divided Self,* was first published in 1958 and the first English translation of *Abel Sánchez* was published only two years before):

> If the patient contrasts his own inner emptiness, worthlessness, *coldness,* desolation, dryness, with the abundance, worth, warmth, companionship that he may yet believe to be elsewhere (a belief which often grows to fantastically idealized proportions, uncorrected as it is by any direct experience), there is evoked a welter of conflicting emotions, from a desperate longing and yearning for what others have

> and he lacks, to frantic envy and hatred of all that is theirs and not his, or a desire to destroy all the goodness, freshness, richness in the world. These feelings may, in turn, be offset by counter-attitudes of disdain, contempt, disgust or indifference.

There are, of course, sources held in common by Unamuno and Laing: these are notably Freud's *Beyond the Pleasure Principle,* Kraepelin's lectures on clinical psychiatry, and Minkowski's writings on psychiatry. But what interests us here is Unamuno's creation of a fictional character who could serve as a clinical case study of pathological envy.

There is another aspect of *Abel Sánchez* that critics have repeatedly pointed out, and that is the oblique but pointed contextualization of the novel within Spain. On his deathbed, Joaquín Monegro sobs: "Why have I been so envious, so bad? What did I do to become that way? What mother's milk did I suck? Was there a philtre, a potion of hate mixed with it? A potion in my blood? Why must I have been born into a country of hatreds? Into a land where the precept seems to be: 'Hate thy neighbor as thyself.' For I have lived hating myself; and here we all live hating ourselves."

Unamuno was a part of the European modernity that dominated thinking and the arts in the aftermath of the Great War, which demolished most of the social standards inherited from the nineteenth century, i.e., god, national state, the class structure. The emphasis shifted to the individual and an exalted freedom to express oneself that surpassed the most extreme individualistic notions of Byron-like romanticism. The threat of military violence was a great risk that was taken without fully comprehending the extent to which humanity was capable of destroying itself. In *Abel Sánchez* the personal hatred and evil of Joaquín, born of his self-hate, is equated with a national psychosis of hate of each other in the Spanish nation. Unamuno had no idea how prophetic his novel was to be. A mere twenty-two years later Spain would plunge into one of the bloodiest and most tragic civil wars, which cost this nation more than a million lives, millions of exiles, and devastation to all aspects of national life. Civil war, therefore, can be seen as the social extension of the symbolic polarity of envy and hatred, which plays out the tragedy of Cain and Abel once again. In the end, both sides lose and it remains for the next generation to attempt to find relationships in place of mutual destruction.

The last of the narratives in this book is unquestionably Unamuno's masterpiece, *San Manuel Bueno, Martyr.* This short novel was the philosophical summing-up of an intense lifetime. Unamuno completed the novel shortly after returning to Salamanca in 1930, after six years spent in exile for his political views on the military dictatorship of Primo de Rivera. It was first published in a popular venue in 1931 and then in book form in 1933, three years before Unamuno's death and the outbreak of the Spanish Civil War. The story is a simple one which has been shared by many other writers: a man of the church loses his faith over the promise of resurrection but nevertheless continues to perform his duties as a priest and to preach the promise of eternal life. Therefore, it is not the relative originality of the story that interests us, but what Unamuno has written into it about life and death, about the community of individuals, and about writing and literature themselves.

The protagonist of the novel is Manuel Bueno, whose life is being narrated by his lifelong disciple, Angela Carballino. With the exception of the last three pages, when Unamuno himself intervenes through an editorial persona, the narration is the confessional, first-person testimony of Angela. The unamunian angst and intense struggle is not only the intimate battle with suicide, it is also the public denial of the struggle. Manuel's life is a constant fight to not surrender to the seduction of death, but it is also an all-out effort to ensure that no one knows this truth and no one discovers the source that is the inquiring mind.

Manuel Bueno, the parish priest of the small lakeside village of Valverde de Lucerna in northeastern Spain, has spent his whole life torn between his desire to reveal himself as a nonbeliever and his desire to conceal this state of mind from others. He finally makes his confession to Angela and her brother Lazarus, but in so doing makes them accomplices in the concealment of the truth from the parishioners. We, the readers, share this problem with Manuel since we are the recipients of Manuel's confession through the confession-like testimony of Angela. The essential point is that as a liar Manuel is irredeemably alone and, therefore, a prime candidate for suicide. He flees solitude and tries to be active all the time, to the point of exhaustion, so as to avoid being alone. Manuel's confession to Lazarus and Angela is a necessity and Angela's confession to us is also necessary. Manuel's confession staves off suicide, and Angela's written confession, which in the eyes of the church will damn her beloved Manuel Bueno, will save his story from oblivion.

Unamuno's characterization of Manuel is masterful. It is because of Manuel's enormous vulnerability to suicide that he has become so adept at concealment. He has mastered the art of leading the community in collective prayer reiterating their faith in eternal life and yet he remains silent himself. All that everyone sees as the perfect parish priest is for the benefit of his parish. He has become a superb actor playing the part of the man he ought to be but is not. If for a moment he would stop pretending to be what he is not and step out of the persona he has come to be in the eyes of the community, he would emerge as Christ—but not as the son of God, but rather as Christ who died on the cross for the love of others. They needed that he make the sacrifice not because of his belief, for he has none; he is a martyr because of his unbelief.

Manuel Bueno's story allows Unamuno to present human truth as an existential truth that is lived out. Manuel's existential truth is neither what he thinks he is nor what others think he is, but rather what he has done, what he has lived. Manuel Bueno lived a life of love for others but not for himself. He lived in loneliness and despair until he took in Angela and her brother as his confidants. Unamuno's Manuel owes much to the sense he developed of the tragic Dane Søren Kierkegaard.

The novel allows the reader to expand the symbolism of snow falling on the lake and melting as Manuel's view of life—a natural cycle in which there is a complete loss of the individual. This symbol is offset by the symbolism of snow falling on the mountain and giving the illusion of continuity and permanence. But Unamuno never allows us to lose sight of Manuel's profound risk. If Manuel experiences himself as a free agent who can choose to live or die, he is open to the possibility of considering his others as *objects* to be saved from his despair. If his others are true subjects with lives of their own, they should also be the agents to decide whether they believe or not. In terms of this existential anxiety, the experience of the other as a person would remove his defense against suicide. It is for this reason that Manuel's relationship with Angela begins as one in which he is both friend and confessor, but, ultimately, it is a relationship between a son and his spiritual mother. Manuel is saved from suicide by his ministry and his living lie, but he is saved from the condemnation of living a lie through his mother-confessor who is his real other—one who is not an object—and it is this subject who saves his memory through her narration.

These three texts by Unamuno move the conflictive space from the social to the interpersonal to the internal conflict of the self. This progressive development was not accidental. Unamuno's probe into the human condition was a search for a philosophy of existence grounded in language as the dwelling place of the human being. What kind of a man was Unamuno? Why did he nurture a contradictory, aggressive, oppositional stance on the issues he discussed and in the characters he created? These questions will never be answered fully, but I can outline the philosophical context that informs the life and writings of Unamuno and, specifically, the three stories in this volume.

At all levels of action, contradiction suggests conflict, whether it is personal or merely a game, but there are certain kinds of contradiction that are, of necessity, conflictual, such as an argument over something claimed by two rivals. If we can expand this commonplace experience to a general discussion of life, we recognize that most people would prefer not to get involved in conflictive contradiction, and those who do would say that it was not the conflict they wanted but rather that their aim was to gain recognition of the validity of their claim from the other party. Unamuno considered life in general to be a continuous oppositional struggle with others, over the rights and property of others and, most important, with the other within. Therefore, even in the case in which a person has no overt opposition in life, there can be opposition from oneself. Unamuno's moral philosophy aimed to reduce appearances to the essential characteristics of what it means to exist as a member of a community without losing one's individuality. As painful as the struggle of Doctor Montarco's conflictive life was to him and his family, it is relatively easy for the reader to set it aside as a rather extreme and eccentric example of small-town narrow-mindedness. The plight of Joaquín Monegro is much more difficult to cope with since it operates in the realm of psychosis, but here also the reader might sense that he or she knows people like Joaquín, although they are the nightmare of human existence that is more internalized than public and, therefore, not fully visible to the other. In fact, we, the readers, know of Joaquín's pathological envy largely because of his diary. San Manuel is almost completely an internal agony like the one Joaquín reveals in his diary. In this case, however, he has not written it himself but confessed to his evangelist Angela Carballino, who narrates the inner conflict. The three stories together stand as significant literary manifestations of a moral philosophy that draws from Kierkegaard and Hegel, as well as from Cervantes and Calderón, and in its expression is indebted to Vico and William James. In the end, Unamuno wrote with an uncommon passion that refused all dogma in a nation of dogmatism.

MARIO J. VALDES
University of Toronto

ABEL SANCHEZ AND OTHER STORIES

ABEL SANCHEZ

The History of a Passion

Following the death of Joaquín Monegro there was found among his papers a kind of memoir of the dark passion which had devoured his life. Fragments taken from this *Confession* (which was the title he gave his journal) are inserted in the following narrative. These fragments serve as a commentary, by Joaquín Monegro himself, on his affliction; they are put in italics.

The *Confession* was addressed to his daughter.

Neither Abel Sanchez nor Joaquín Monegro could remember a time when they had not known each other. They had known each other since before childhood—since earliest infancy, in fact; for their nursemaids often met and brought the two infants together even before the children knew how to talk. They had each learned about each other as they learned about themselves.

Thus had they grown up, friends from birth, and treated almost as brothers in their upbringing.

In their walks, in their games, in their mutual friendships it was Joaquín, the more willful of the two, who seemed to initiate and dominate everything. Still, Abel, who appeared always to yield, always did as he pleased. The truth was that he found not obeying more important than commanding. The two almost never quarreled. "As far as I'm concerned, it's whatever you want. . . . " Abel would say to Joaquín, who would become exasperated; for by this "whatever you want . . ." Abel managed to show his disdain of the argument.

"You never say no!" Joaquín would burst out.

"What's the use?"

"Well, now," Joaquín began one day when they were with some comrades who were preparing to take a walk, "this fellow"—pointing at Abel—"doesn't want to go to the pine grove."

"Me?" yelled Abel. "Who said I don't want to? Of course I want to. It's really up to you. Yes! Yes! Let's go there!"

"No! It's not whatever I want. I've told you that before. It's not whatever I want. The fact is that you don't want to go!"

"I do, I tell you!"

"In that case *I* don't want to."

"Then I don't either."

"That's not fair"; by now Joaquín was screaming. To the other boys he yelled: "Either go with him or come with me!"

And they all went with Abel, leaving Joaquín to himself.

When Joaquín went to comment, in his *Confession,* on this event of their infancy, he wrote:

> "Already Abel was, unconsciously, the congenial one, and I the antipathetic one, without my knowing why this was so any better than he did. I was left alone. Ever since childhood my friends left me to myself."

All during their secondary school studies, which they pursued together, Joaquín was the incubator and hatcher, hotly in pursuit of prizes. Joaquín was first in the classroom; Abel was first outside class, in the patio of the Institute, and among his comrades, in the street, in the country, and whenever they played hooky. It was Abel who made everyone laugh with his natural cleverness; he was especially applauded for his caricature of the professors. "Joaquín is much more diligent, but Abel is quicker . . . if he were only to study. . . ." And this prevailing judgment on the part of his classmates, of which Joaquín was aware, served to poison his heart further. He was soon tempted to neglect his studies and strive to excel over Abel in his own field; but he managed to tell himself: "Bah!

What do they know. . . ." And in the end he remained faithful to his own nature. Besides, however much he attempted to surpass the other in natural facility or grace, he was unsuccessful. His jokes were not greeted with laughter, and he was considered fundamentally serious and was thought to be basically cold. "You're really macabre," Federico Cuadrado would say to him, "those jokes of yours would do well at a wake."

The two of them finished their schooling. Abel embarked on an artist's career and began the study of painting; Joaquín entered medical school. They saw each other frequently and spoke of the progress each was making in his respective studies. Often Joaquín would endeavor to prove to Abel that medicine, too, was an art, a fine art even, to which poetic inspiration was native. On other occasions, however, Joaquín denigrated the fine arts, enervators of the will, and extolled science, which "elevated, fortified and expanded the spirit with Truth."

"The truth is that medicine is not actually a science," from Abel. "It is more like an art, a professional practice based on the sciences."

"But I don't intend to dedicate myself to ministering the sick."

"A very honorable and practical ministry. . . ."

"Yes, but not for me," interrupted Joaquín.

"It may be altogether as honorable and practical as you like, but I detest such honorableness and practicality. Making money by taking a pulse, looking at tongues, and writing some kind of prescription is for others. I aspire to something higher."

"Higher?"

"Yes. I hope to open new pathways. I expect to devote myself to scientific investigation. The glory of medicine belongs to those who discover the secret of some disease, not to those who apply the discovery with greater or lesser luck."

"It's a pleasure to see you in this idealistic frame of mind."

"Oh, do you suppose that only you people, the artists, the painters, dream of glory?"

"Wait now, no one said that I dream of any such thing. . . ."

"No? In that case why have you taken up painting?"

"Because, if one is successful, it's a profession which promises. . . ."

"What does it promise?"

"Well, now, it promises . . . money."

"Throw that bone to some other dog, Abel. I've known you ever since we were born, almost. You can't tell that to me. I know you."

"And have I ever tried to deceive you?"

"No, but you deceive without trying. Despite

your air of not caring about anything, of acting as if life were a game, you're really terribly ambitious."

"Ambitious, me?"

"Yes, ambitious for glory, fame, renown. . . . You always were, you have been since birth, even though you conceal it."

"Wait a bit, Joaquín, and tell me something. Did I ever dispute your prizes with you? Weren't you always first in your class, the 'most promising'?"

"Yes, but the little cock of the walk, the one everybody humored, was you. . . ."

"And what could I do about that?"

"Do you want me to believe that you weren't seeking that kind of popularity?"

"Now, if *you* had sought it. . . ."

"If I had sought it? I despise the masses!"

"All right, all right. Spare me the speech and the nonsense, and save yourself the bother, too. It would be better if you talked about your girl friend again."

"My girl friend?"

"Well, your little cousin, then, whom you'd like to make your girl friend."

Joaquín was, in fact, attempting to storm the heart of his cousin Helena and was displaying all the ardor of his intense and jealous nature in the amorous engagement. And he unburdened himself—the inevitable and salubrious unburdening of the embattled lover—to his confidant and friend, Abel.

How his cousin Helena made him suffer!

"Each time I see her I understand her less," he would complain to Abel. "That girl is like a sphinx to me."

"You know what Oscar Wilde said: every woman is a sphinx without a secret."

"Well, Helena seems to have one. She must be in love with someone else, even though the other doesn't know it. I'm certain she's in love with someone else."

"Why do you think so?"

"Otherwise I can't explain her attitude toward me."

"You mean that because she doesn't want to love you, want you as a lover . . . for as a cousin she probably loves you. . . ."

"Don't make fun of me!"

"Well then, because she doesn't want you for a lover, or more exactly, for a husband, she must be in love with someone else? Nice logic!"

"I understand what I'm saying."

"Yes, and I understand you, too."

"You?"

"Don't you claim to be the one who understands *me* best? Why is it surprising if I claim to understand you? We met at the same time."

"In any case, I'm telling you that this woman is driving me mad. She'll drive me too far. She's playing with me. If she had said no from the beginning, it would have been all right; but to keep me in suspense, telling me that she'll see, that she'll think it over. . . . These things can't be thought over, coquette that she is!"

"She's probably studying you."

"Studying me? Her? What is there about me to study? What *could* she study?"

"Joaquín, Joaquín, you're underestimating yourself and underestimating her. Or do you think that she has only to see you, and hear you, know that you love her, in order to surrender herself to you?"

"Oh, I know, I've always aroused antipathy. . . ."

"Come, now, don't get yourself into that state. . . ."

"It's just that this woman is playing with me. And it's not honorable to play this way with a man who is sincere, loyal and above-board. . . . If you could only see how beautiful she is! And the colder and more disdainful she grows, the more beautiful she becomes! There are times when I don't know if I love her more or hate her more. . . . Would you like me to introduce you to her . . . ?"

"Well, if you . . ."

"Good, I'll introduce you."

"And if she wants . . ."

"What?"

"I'll paint her portrait."

"That's wonderful!"

But that night Joaquín slept badly, envisioning the portrait and haunted by the idea that Abel Sanchez, the guileless charmer, the one who was humored in everything, was going to paint Helena's portrait.

What would come of it? Would Helena, too, like all their mutual friends, find Abel the more endearing? He thought of calling off the introduction, but, since he had already promised. . . .

CHAPTER 2

"What did you think of my cousin?" Joaquín asked Abel the day after the two had been introduced. Abel had broached the matter of the portrait to Helena, and she had received the proposal with extreme satisfaction.

"Well now, do you want the truth?"

"The truth at all times, Abel. If we told each other the truth always, this world would be Paradise."

"Yes, and if each one told himself the truth. . . ."

"Well, the truth then!"

"The truth is that your cousin and future sweetheart, perhaps wife, Helena, seems to me a peacock. . . . I mean a female peacock. . . . You understand what I mean . . . ?"

"Yes, I understand you."

"Since I don't know how to express myself well except with a brush. . . ."

"And so you'll paint this peacock, this female peacock, as it spreads its train, the tail feathers decorated with eyes, the little head piece. . . ."

"As a model, she's excellent! Really excellent, my friend! What eyes! What a mouth! A mouth both full and formed . . . eyes which do not quite look at you . . . and what a neck! Above all, what color, what complexion! If you will not be offended. . . ."

"Offended?"

"I will tell you that she has the color of a wild Indian, or, better still, of an untamed animal. There is something of the panther about her, in the best sense, and she is so totally indifferent to it all, so cold."

"So cold!"

"Anyway, old man, I expect to paint you a stupendous portrait."

"Paint me a portrait? You mean paint *her* a portrait."

"No, the portrait shall be for you, even if it is of her."

"No! The portrait will be for her."

"Well, then, for the two of you. Who knows. . . . Perhaps it will join you together."

"Ah! Why, of course, since from being a portrait painter you take on the role of. . . ."

"Whatever you want, Joaquín, a go-between if you like, as long as you stop suffering as you have. It's painful for me to see you in that state."

The painting sessions began, the three of them assembling for the occasion. Helena would take her seat, solemn and cold, in an attitude of disdain, like a goddess borne along by destiny. "May I talk?" she asked on the first day, and Abel answered her: "Yes, you can talk and move about; it's better for me, in fact, if you do move about and talk, for in that way the features take on life. . . . This will not be a photograph, and besides I don't want you like a statue." And so she talked and talked, but without moving very much, careful of her posture. What did she talk of? The two men were not aware. Because both of them devoured her with their eyes; they saw her, but they did not hear. . . .

And she talked and talked, considering it a sign of good manners not to remain silent; and, whenever possible, she taunted Joaquín.

"Are you having any luck getting patients, little cousin?" she would ask.

"Do you really care about that?"

"Of course I care about it. You think I don't. . . . Imagine . . ."

"No, I can't imagine."

"Since you interest yourself so much in me, I couldn't do less than interest myself in your affairs. And besides, who knows. . . ."

"Who knows what?"

"All right, let's leave the subject," Abel interrupted. "You both don't do anything but scold."

"It's natural," Helena said, "between relatives. . . . And besides, they say that's the way it begins."

"What begins?" Joaquín asked.

"That's something you must know, since you began it."

"What I'm going to do now is finish!"

"Well, there are various ways of finishing something, cousin."

"And various ways of beginning."

"No doubt. Tell me, Abel, do I disarrange myself with this *badinage?*"

"No, no, on the contrary. This *badinage,* as you call it, adds some expression to your look and gesture. But . . ."

Within two days Abel and Helena were addressing each other familiarly; on the third day, Joaquín, who had wanted it this way, missed the painting session.

"Let me see how it looks now," Helena said getting up to stand before the portrait.

"What do you think?"

"I'm not an expert and besides I'm not the one to judge whether or not it's like me."

"What? Don't you have a mirror? Haven't you looked at yourself in it?"

"Yes, but . . ."

"But what . . . ?"

"Oh, I don't know. . . ."

"Don't you see that you're quite stunning?"

"Don't be a flatterer."

"Well then, we'll ask Joaquín."

"Don't speak of him to me, if you please. What a bore!"

"Well, it's of him that I must speak to you."

"Then I'm going. . . ."

"No, listen! What you're doing to that boy is very bad."

"Oh! So now you're going to plead his case for him? Is this business about the portrait simply an excuse?"

"Look, Helena, it isn't right for you to act this way, playing with your cousin. He's something, after all, something . . ."

"Yes, he's insufferable!"

"No, he's engrossed in himself, he's proud, stubborn, full of his own importance, but he's also good, honorable in every respect, intelligent; a brilliant future in his profession is ahead of him; he loves you passionately. . . ."

"And if in spite of all that I don't love him . . . ?"

"Then in that case you should discourage him."

"And haven't I discouraged him enough? I'm tired of telling him that I think he's a good fellow, but for that very reason, because he does strike me as a good fellow, a good cousin, a good 'coz'—and I'm not using the word nastily—I really don't want him for a suitor and for everything that comes later."

"But he says. . . ."

"If he has told you anything else, Abel, he hasn't told you the truth. Can I send him on his way or forbid him from speaking to me since he is, after all, my cousin. Cousin! What a joke!"

"Don't be so mocking."

"The fact is I can't. . . ."

"Moreover, he suspects something else. He insists on making himself believe that since you don't want to love him, you are secretly enamored of someone else. . . ."

"Has he told you that?"

"Yes, he has told me just that."

Helena bit her lips, blushed, and was silent for a moment.

"Yes, he told me that," Abel repeated, letting his right hand rest on the maulstick which he held against the canvas; he was gazing steadily at Helena, as if he wanted to find a meaning in some feature of her face.

"Well, if he insists. . . ."

"What . . . ?"

"He'll succeed in having me fall in love with someone else. . . ."

Abel painted no more that afternoon. And the two became lovers.

CHAPTER 3

Abel's portrait of Helena was a tremendous success. There was always someone standing before the show window where it was exhibited. "Another great painter among us," it was said. And Helena made a point of passing near the place where her portrait was hanging in order to hear the comments, and she strolled through the streets of the city like an immortal portrait imbued with life, like a work of art with a full train. Had she been born perhaps for just this?

Joaquín scarcely slept.

"She's worse than ever," he told Abel. "She's really playing with me now. She'll be my death."

"Naturally. She's become a professional beauty. . . ."

"Yes, you've immortalized her. Another Gioconda!"

"And still, you, as a doctor, can do more, you can lengthen her life. . . ."

"Or shorten it."

"Don't act so tragic."

"What am I going to do, Abel, what am I going to do . . . ?"

"Learn to have patience. . . ."

"And then, she has told me certain things

from which I gather you told her of my feeling that she is in love with somebody else. . . ."

"It was in order to help your cause. . . ."

"To help my cause . . . Abel, Abel, you're working with her . . . the two of you are deceiving me. . . ."

"Deceiving you? In what way? Has she promised you anything?"

"And you, has she promised *you* anything?"

"Is she your mistress, perhaps?"

"Is she already *yours* then?"

Abel kept quiet, and changed color.

"You see," exclaimed Joaquín, trembling and beginning to stammer, "you see?"

"See what?"

"Will you deny it now? Are you brazen faced enough to deny it to me?"

"Well, Joaquín, we have been friends since before we knew each other, almost brothers. . . ."

"And a brother is to be treacherously stabbed, is that it?"

"Don't get so furious. Show some patience. . . ."

"Patience? And what has my life been if not a continuous show of patience, continuous suffering? . . . You, the most attractive, the most pampered, the constant victor, the artist . . . And I . . ."

Tears sprang from his eyes and cut short his words.

"And what was I to do, Joaquín, what did you want me to do?"

"Not to have courted her, since it was I who loved her!"

"But it was she, Joaquín, it was she. . . ."

"And naturally it is you, the fortunate one, the artist, the favorite of fortune, you who women court. Well now you have her. . . ."

"She has me, you mean."

"Yes, the female peacock, the professional beauty, the Gioconda, now she has you. . . . You will be her painter. . . . You will paint her in every posture and every light, clothed and unclothed. . . ."

"Joaquín!"

"And so you will immortalize her. She will live as long as your paintings live. Or rather, not *live*—for Helena doesn't live; but endure, and will endure like marble, the marble of which she is made. For she is made of stone, cold and hard like you. A mass of flesh!"

"Don't get into such a rage."

"Oh, I shouldn't get into a rage, you think, I shouldn't be enraged? This is an infamous piece of work you've accomplished, a low, vile trick."

He felt weak and disheartened, however, and grew quiet, as if words with which to match the violence of his passion failed him.

"But stop and consider," Abel said in his most dulcet voice, which was also his most terrible.

"Was I going to make her love you, if she doesn't want to love you? She doesn't think of you as her. . . ."

"No, of course not, I'm not attractive to any woman; I was born already condemned."

"I swear to you, Joaquín. . . ."

"Don't bother with oaths."

"I swear to you that if it were up to me alone, Helena would be your beloved now, and tomorrow she would be your wife. If I were able to give her up to you. . . ."

"You'd trade her to me for a mess of potage, is that it?"

"Trade her, no! I would give her up freely and would be more than happy in seeing you both happy, but. . . ."

"I know, she does not love me, and she does love you, isn't that it?"

"That's true."

"She rejects me, who wanted her, and wants you, who rejected her."

"Exactly. Although you won't believe me, it's I who was seduced."

"Oh, what a way of putting on airs! You nauseate me!"

"Airs?"

"Yes. To play the role of the one seduced is worse than playing the seducer. Poor victim! Women fight over you. . . ."

"Don't exasperate me, Joaquín. . . ."

"You? Exasperate *you?* I tell you this is a vile trick, a piece of infamy, a crime. . . . We are through with each other forever!"

But then later, changing his tone, and with fathomless sorrow in his voice:

"Have compassion on me, Abel, have compassion. Don't you see that everyone looks at me askance, that everyone is opposed to me. . . . You are young, fortunate, indulged; there are more than enough women for you. . . . Let me have Helena; you can be sure I won't be able to love another. . . . Let me have Helena. . . ."

"But I already yield her to you. . . ."

"Make her listen to me; make her acknowledge me; make her understand that I am dying for her, that without her I can't live. . . ."

"You don't know her. . . ."

"Yes, I know you both! But, for God's sake, swear to me that you will not marry her. . . ."

"Who spoke of marriage?"

"Ah, then all this is only to make me jealous? It's true that she is nothing but a coquette . . . worse than a coquette, a . . ."

"Be quiet!" roared Abel.

His voice had been such that Joaquín remained silent, staring at him.

"It's impossible, Joaquín; one cannot deal with you. You are impossible."

And Abel turned and walked away.

I passed a horrible night—Joaquín wrote in the *Confession* he left behind—*tossing from one side of the bed to the other, biting the pillow spasmodically, and getting up to drink water from the washstand pitcher. I ran a fever. From time to time I drowsed off into bitter dreams. I thought of killing both of them, and I made mental calculations—as if it were a matter of a drama or novel I was creating—planning the details of my bloody vengeance, and I composed imaginary dialogues with the two of them. It seemed to me that Helena had only wanted to affront me, nothing more; that she had made love to Abel to slight me, but that in reality—pure mass of flesh before a mirror that she was—she could not love anybody. And I desired her more than ever and more furiously than before. During one of the interminable half-waking, half-sleeping spells of that night I dreamt that I possessed her beside the cold and inert body of Abel. That night was a tempest of evil desires, of rage, of vile appetites, of futile wrath. With daylight and the weariness of so much suffering, reason returned to me and I understood that I had no right whatsoever to Helena. But I began to hate Abel with all my soul, and, at the same time, to plan the concealment of this loathing, which I would cultivate and tend deep down in my soul's entrails. Loathing, did I say? I did not yet want to give it a name. Nor did I care to understand that I had been born predestined to bear the weight of hatred upon me and its seed within me. That night I was born into my life's hell.*

CHAPTER 4

"Helena," Abel addressed her, "the incident with Joaquín disturbs my sleep. . . ."

"The incident? Why should it?"

"I wonder what will happen when I tell him we plan to be married. . . . Still, he seems to have quieted down and more or less resigned himself to our relationship. . . ."

"He's a fine example of resignation!"

"The truth is that what we did wasn't altogether well done."

"What? You, too? Are women supposed to be like animals, to be handed round and loaned out and rented and sold?"

"No, but . . ."

"But, what?"

"Well, it was he who introduced me to you, so I could paint your portrait, and I took advantage. . . ."

"And that was well done! Was I, by any chance, engaged to him? And even if I had been! Everyone must go his own way."

"Yes, but . . ."

"But what? Are you sorry after all? Well, as far as I'm concerned. . . . Even if you were to leave me now, now that I'm promised to you and everyone knows that you will ask permission to marry me one of these days, even then I wouldn't want Joaquín. No! I'd want him less than ever. I would have more than enough suitors, more of them than fingers on my hand, like this,"—and here she raised her two long hands with their tapering fingers, those hands which Abel had painted with so much love, and she shook her fingers so that they fluttered.

Abel seized her two hands in his own strong ones, carried them to his mouth, and kissed them at great length. And then her mouth. . . .

"Be quiet, Abel!"

"You're right, Helena, we must not undermine our happiness by thinking of what poor Joaquín feels and suffers on account of it. . . ."

"Poor Joaquín? He's nothing but an envious wretch!"

"Still, Helena, there are states of envy. . . ."

"Let him go to the devil!"

After a pause filled with black silence:

"Well, we'll invite him to the wedding. . . ."

"Helena!"

"What harm would there be in that? He's my cousin, and your first friend; we owe to him the fact that we know each other. And if you don't invite him, I will. He won't go? So much the better! He will go? Better than ever!"

CHAPTER 5

When Abel told Joaquín of his impending marriage, the latter said:

"It had to be. Each to his own."

"Now, you must understand. . . ."

"Yes, I understand; don't think me demented or mad; I understand; it's all right; I hope you will be happy. . . . I can never be so again. . . ."

"But, Joaquín, for God's sake, in the name of everything you love most. . . ."

"That's enough. Let's not speak of it any further. Make Helena happy, and may she make you happy, too. . . . I have already forgiven you. . . ."

"Have you truly?"

"Yes, truly. I want to forgive you. I will try to make my own life."

"Then I will venture to invite you to the wedding, in my name . . ."

"And in hers too? . . ."

"In hers too."

"I understand. I will go in order to heighten your happiness. I'll go."

As a wedding gift, Joaquín sent Abel a brace of magnificent damascened pistols, worthy of an artist.

"They're for you to shoot yourself in the head with, when you grow weary of me," Helena told her future husband.

"What are you talking about, woman? What an idea!"

"Who knows his intentions . . . ? He spends his life plotting."

In the days following the day when he told me they were to be married,—Joaquín wrote in his *Confession—I felt as if my soul had frozen. And the icy cold pressed upon my heart, as if flames of ice were suffocating me. I had trouble breathing. My hatred for Helena, and even more, for Abel—and hatred it was, a cold hatred whose roots choked my heart—had become like a petrified growth, as hard as stone. Yet, it was not so much a poisonous plant as it was an iceberg which blocked up my soul; or rather, my soul itself was congealed in hatred. The ice of it was so crystalline that I could see into and through it with complete clarity. I was perfectly well aware that they were right, absolutely right, and that I had no right whatever to Helena; that one ought not, cannot, force a woman's love; that since they loved each other, they should be united. And still, confusedly I felt that it had been I who had brought them, not only together, but to the point of love; that they had come together because they both wished to spurn me; that Helena's decision was largely determined by an urge to see me suffer and rage, to make me set my teeth on edge, to humiliate me before Abel; on his part I sensed a supreme egotism which never allowed him to take notice of the suffering of others. Ingenuously, he simply did not pay any attention to the existence of others. The rest of us were, at most, models for his paintings. He did not even hate, so full of himself was he.*

I attended the wedding, my soul frost-bitten with hatred, my heart coated with bitter ice, and seized with the apprehension, the mortal terror, that when I heard their "I do," the ice would crack, and my heart would break, and I would die then and there, or turn into an idiot. I went to the wedding as one goes to one's death. And what happened was more mortal than death itself; it was worse, much worse than dying. I wish I might have died instead.

She was completely beautiful. When she greeted me I felt as if an icy sword was plunged into the ice which froze my heart; it was her insolent smile of compassion which cut through me. "Thank you," she said; "poor Joaquín." I understood. As for Abel, I do not know whether he even really saw me. "I understand your sacrifice," he said, merely to say something. "No, no," I hastened to say, "there is none involved; I told you I would come and I came; you see how reasonable I am; I could not have failed my eternal friend, my brother." My attitude must have seemed interesting to him, though scarcely very picturesque. I was like the Comendador *in Don Juan, a guest made of stone.*

As the fatal moment drew near I began to count the seconds. "In a very short time," I told myself, "everything is over for me." I believe my heart stopped. Clearly and distinctly I heard each "Yes," his and hers. She looked at me as she uttered the word. And I grew colder than ever, not through any sudden clutching at my heart or any palpitation, but rather as if what I heard did not concern me. This very fact filled me with an infernal terror and fear of myself. I felt myself to be worse than a monster; I felt as if I did not exist, as if I were nothing more than a piece of ice, and as if this would be true forever. I went so far as to touch my skin, to pinch myself, to take my pulse. "Am I really alive? Am I myself?" I asked myself.

I do not wish to recall everything that happened that day. They took leave of me and started out on their honeymoon voyage. I sank myself in my books, in my studies, in my practice, for I was beginning to have one. The mental clarity which resulted from this irreparable blow, the discovery within myself that there is no soul, moved me to seek in study, not consolation—consolation I neither needed nor wanted—but instead the basis for an immense ambition. I must henceforth crush with the fame of my name the fame, already growing, of Abel. My scientific discoveries, a work of art in their own way, of true poetry, must put his paintings in the shade. Helena must one day come to realize that it was I, the medical man, the antipathetic one, who could surround her with an aureole of glory, and not he, not this painter. I plunged headlong into my studies. I even went so far as to believe I might forget the newly-wedded pair! I wished to turn science into a narcotic, at the same time that I used it as a stimulant.

CHAPTER 6

A short while after the couple returned from their honeymoon, Abel fell gravely ill, and Joaquín was summoned to examine and attend him.

"I am very worried, Joaquín," Helena told him; "he was delirious all night; in his delirium he called for you constantly."

Joaquín examined his friend with every care and attention, and then, looking fixedly at his cousin, he told her:

"It's a serious matter, but I think I will be able to save him. It's I for whom there is no salvation."

"Yes, save him for me," she exclaimed. "And you know that . . ."

"Yes, I know!" And Joaquín took his leave.

Helena hurried to her husband's bedside, and laid her hand on her husband's forehead. He was burning with fever, and Helena began to tremble. "Joaquín, Joaquín," Abel called out in his delirium, "forgive us, forgive me!"

"Be quiet," Helena exclaimed, bending almost to his ear, "be quiet; he's come to see you and says he will cure you, that he will make you well. . . . He says you should be quiet. . . ."

"He'll cure me? . . ." the sick man repeated mechanically.

When Joaquín arrived at his house he, too, was feverish, with a kind of icy fever. "And if he should die? . . ." he thought to himself. He threw himself on the bed fully dressed, and began to imagine what would happen if Abel were to die: Helena's mourning, his own meetings and conversation with the widow, her remorse, her discovery of his true character and of his burning desire to revenge the wrong done him, of his violent need of her, of her falling into his arms at last in the realization that her other life, her treason, had been only a nightmare, the bad dream of a coquette; she would know that she had always loved him, Joaquín, and no other. "But he will not die," he told himself. "I will not let him die, I must not let him, my honor is at stake, and . . . I need to have him live! He must live!"

And as he said "he must live!" his soul trembled, just as the foliage of an oak trembles in the upheaval of a storm.

They were atrocious days, those days of Abel's sickness—Joaquín wrote in the *Confession—days of incredible torture. It was in my power to let him die without anyone suspecting, without leaving any telltale evidence behind. In the course of my practice I have known strange cases of mysterious death which later I have seen illumi-*

nated in the tragic light of subsequent events, as, by the remarriage of the widow, or like developments. I struggled then, as I had never struggled with myself before, against that foul dragon which has poisoned and darkened my life. My honor as a doctor was at stake, my honor as a man, and my mental well-being, my sanity itself was involved. I understood that I struggled in the clutches of madness; I saw the spectre of insanity and felt its shadow across my heart. But in the end, I conquered. I saved Abel from death. I never worked more fortunately, more accurately. My excess of unhappiness allowed me to be most happy and correct in my diagnosis.

"Your . . . husband is completely out of danger," Joaquín reported to Helena one day.

"Thank you, Joaquín, thank you." She grasped him by the hand; and he permitted his hand to rest in her two hands. "You don't know how much we owe you. . . ."

"And you don't know how much I owe you both. . . ."

"For God's sake, don't act that way . . . Now that we owe you so much, let's not go back to that other again. . . ."

"No, I am not returning to anything else. I owe you a good deal. This illness of Abel's has taught me much, really a great deal. . . ."

"Ah, you look on it as one more case?"

"No, no, Helena; it's I who am the case!"

"But, I don't understand you."

"Nor do I, completely. And yet, I can tell you that in these days of fighting to save your husband. . . ."

"Say 'Abel,' call him by his name!"

"Very well; fighting for his life, then, I studied my own sickness along with his, and decided . . . to marry!"

"Ah! But do you have the girl?"

"No, not yet, but I will find her. I need a home. I will look for a wife. Or, do you think, Helena, that I will not find a woman to love me?"

"Of course you will find her, of course you will!"

"A woman who will love me, I mean."

"Yes, I understand, a woman who will love you, yes!"

"Because as far as a good match is concerned . . ."

"Yes, there is no question but that you are a good match . . . young, not poor, a good career ahead of you, beginning to make a name, good and kind. . . ."

"Good . . . yes, and unappealing, isn't that so?"

"No, no, not at all; you're not lacking appeal."

"Oh, Helena, Helena, where shall I find another woman?"

". . . who will love you?"

"No, who will simply not deceive me, who will tell me the truth, who will not mock me, Helena, who will not mock me! . . . Who may marry me from desperation, perhaps, merely because I will support her, but who will tell me. . . ."

"You were quite right when you said you were ill, Joaquín. You should marry!"

"And do you think, Helena, that there is anyone, man or woman, who might love me?"

"There is no one who cannot find someone to love him."

"And will I love my wife? Will I be able to love her? Tell me."

"Why, nothing would be more likely. . . ."

"Because, really, Helena, the worst is not to be unloved, or to lack the faculty to be loved; the worst is not to be able to love."

"That's what Don Mateo, the parish priest, says about the devil, that he cannot love."

"And the devil is right here on earth, Helena."

"Be quiet; don't say such things."

"It's worse for me to say them to myself."

"Then be quiet altogether!"

CHAPTER 7

For his own salvation, and in the need to assuage his passion, Joaquín devoted himself to searching for a woman, for the arms of a wife where he might take refuge from the hatred he felt, a lap where he might hide his head, like a child afraid of the dark, afraid to look at the hellish eyes of the ice-dragon.

Then, the poor unfortunate woman named Antonia!

Antonia had been born to be a mother; she was all tenderness and compassion. With superb instinct, she divined the invalid in Joaquín, a man sick of soul, possessed; and, without knowing why, she fell in love with his misfortune. The cold, curt words of the doctor who had no faith in the goodness of others exercised a mysterious attraction for her.

Antonia was the only daughter of a widow who was being treated by Joaquín. "Will my mother come through this crisis?" she asked Joaquín.

"It's a very difficult case, very difficult. The poor little woman is very tired, very run down; she must have suffered a good deal. . . . Her heart is very weak. . . ."

"Save her, Don Joaquín, save her! If I could, I would give my life for hers."

"That cannot be done. Besides, who knows? Your own life, Antonia, may be more needed than hers. . . ."

"My life? For what? For whom?"

"Who knows! . . ."

The death of the poor widow occurred inevitably.

"It could not have been otherwise, Antonia," Joaquín told her. "Science is powerless."

"Yes, God wished it so."

"God?"

"Ah!" exclaimed Antonia, her eyes fastening on the dry, steely-eyed face of Joaquín; "you don't believe in God?"

"I? . . . I don't know! . . ."

The sharp twinge of pity which the unfortunate orphan felt for the doctor momentarily made her forget the death of her mother.

"If I did not believe in Him, what would I do now?"

"Life finds answers for everything, Antonia."

"Death finds more! And now . . . so much alone . . . without anyone . . ."

"That's so, solitude can be terrible. But you have the memory of your holy mother, and a life to devote to commending her to God. . . . There is a solitude much more terrible!"

"What is it?"

"The solitude of a person who all despise, whom everyone mocks. . . . The solitude of a person to whom no one will tell the truth."

"And what truth is it that you want to be told?"

"Would you tell me the truth, now, at this moment, over the still-warm body of your mother? Would you swear to tell me the truth?"

"Yes, I would tell you the truth."

"Good . . . I am an antipathetic person, isn't that so?"

"No; that is not so!"

"The truth, Antonia . . ."

"No; it isn't so."

"Well, then, what am I? . . ."

"You? You are an unfortunate, a man who suffers. . . ."

The ice in Joaquín began to melt and tears came to his eyes. Once again he trembled to the roots of his soul.

It was not very long afterwards that Joaquín and the recent orphan became engaged, planning to marry as soon as her year of mourning was over.

My poor little wife—Joaquín was to write years later in his *Confession*—*she struggled to love me and cure me, to overcome the repugnance that I must have aroused in her. She never told me this, she never even let it be understood. But, could I have failed to arouse repugnance in her especially when I revealed to her the leprosy of my soul, the gangrene of my hatred? She married me as she would have married a leper—I have no doubt of this at all—from motives of pity, a divine pity, and from a Christian spirit of abnegation and self-sacrifice, in order to save my soul, and thereby save her own. She married me out of the heroism of saintliness. And she was a saint! . . . But she did not cure me of Helena, and she did not cure me of Abel. Her saintliness was for me just one more source of remorse.*

Her gentleness irritated me. There were times when—God forgive me!—I would have wished her wicked, hot-tempered, disdainful.

CHAPTER 8

Meanwhile Abel's fame as an artist continued to spread. He had become one of the most renowned painters of the entire nation, and his name was making itself known across the border. And this growing fame affected Joaquín like the desolation of a hailstorm. "Yes, he is a very *scientific* painter; he is a master of technique; he knows a good deal, a good deal; he is exceedingly clever"; thus spoke Joaquín of his friend, in words that somehow hissed. It was a way of seeming to praise him, by denigrating him.

Because, in truth, it was Joaquín who presumed to be the artist; a true poet in his profession, a diagnostician of genius, creative, intuitive; he even dreamed of abandoning his clientele in order to dedicate himself to pure science, to theoretical pathology, to research. But, then, he was earning so much! . . .

And yet, it was not profit—he wrote in his posthumous *Confession—which most prevented me from devoting myself to scientific investigation. On the one hand, I was drawn to it by a desire to become renowned, to build a great scientific reputation which would overshadow Abel's artistic fame and thereby humiliate Helena, revenging myself on them both, and on everybody else as well—it was my wildest hope. On the other hand, this same murky passion, this extravagant grudge and hatred, deprived me of all serenity of soul. No, I did not have the will to study, the pure and tranquil spirt which was necessary. My practice distracted me, moreover.*

My practice distracted me, and yet there were times when I trembled, thinking that my state of inner distraction prevented me from paying the strict attention required by the ills of my poor patients.

Then occurred a case which shook me to my foundations. I was attending a poor woman, who was rather dangerously, but still not desperately, ill. Abel had made a portrait of her; a magnificent portrait, one of his best, one of those which have remained as definitive among his works. And it was this painting which was this first thing that came into my sight—and into my hate—as soon as I entered the sick woman's home. In the portrait she was alive, more alive than in her bed of suffering flesh and bone. And the portrait seemed to say to me: Look, he has given me life forever! Let's see if you can prolong this other, earthly life of mine! At the bedside of the poor invalid, as I listened to her heart and took her pulse, I was obsessed by the other woman, the painted one. I was stupefied, completely stupefied, and as a result the poor woman died on me; or rather, I let her die, in my stupe-

faction, in my criminal distraction. I was convulsed with horror at myself, my miserable self.

A few days after the woman's death, I found it necessary to go to her house to visit still another sick member of the family, and I entered firmly resolved not to look at the portrait. But it was useless, for the portrait looked at me, regardless of whether or not I looked at it, and it drew my gaze perforce. As I took my leave, the recently bereaved husband accompanied me to the door. We paused at the foot of the portrait, and I, as if I had been impelled by some irresistible and fatal force, exclaimed:

"A magnificent portrait! It is one of the greatest things Abel has done."

"Yes," answered the widower, "it is the greatest consolation left me now. I gaze at it for hours. It seems to speak to me."

"Oh yes, yes," I added, "Abel is a stupendous artist!"

As I went out, I said to myself: "I let her die, and he resurrected her!"

Joaquín suffered a great deal whenever one of his patients died, especially if they were children; the deaths of certain others, however, left him almost entirely unaffected. "Why should such a one want to live . . . ?" he would ask himself about someone. "I would actually be doing him a favor to let him die. . . ."

His powers of observation as a psychologist

had grown sharper as his spirit languished, and he was quick to intuit the most hidden moral lacerations. He perceived, behind all the falsity of convention, how husbands foresaw the death of their wives without any sorrow whatever—when they did not consciously desire it—and how wives longed to be free of their husbands, longed even to take other husbands already chosen beforehand. In the same year in which a patient named Alvarez died, his widow married Menéndez, the dead man's dear friend, and Joaquín said to himself: "That death was really quite strange. . . . Only now do I see it all clearly. . . . Humanity is absolutely vile! And that lady is a 'charitable' lady, one of the most 'honorable' ladies. . . ."

"Doctor," one of his patients said to him once, "for God's sake, will you kill me? Kill me without telling me anything, for I cannot go on. . . . Give me something which will make me sleep forever. . . ."

"And why should I not do what this man wants me to do," Joaquín asked himself, "if he lives only to suffer? It makes me grieve! What a filthy world!"

His patients were not infrequently mirrors for him.

One day a poor woman of the neighborhood came to see him; she was wasted by her years and work, and her husband, after 25 years of marriage, had formed a liaison with a miserable adventuress. The rejected woman had come to tell the doctor her troubles.

"Ay, Don Joaquín! Let us see if you, who are said to know so much, can give me a remedy to cure my poor husband of the philter which this loose woman has given him."

"But what philter, my good woman?"

"He is going to go and live with her; he is leaving me, after twenty-five years. . . ."

"It would have been even stranger if he had left you when you were a newly-married pair, while you were still young and even . . ."

"Oh, no sir, no! The fact is that she has given him some kind of love potion which has turned his head. Otherwise, it just could not be . . . it could not be. . . ."

"A love potion," murmured Joaquín, "a love potion? . . ."

"Yes, Don Joaquín; yes, a love potion. . . . And you, who have so much knowledge, let me have some sort of remedy against it."

"Ah, my good woman, the ancients have already searched in vain to find a liquor which would rejuvenate. . . ."

And when the poor woman went away in desolation, Joaquín said to himself: "But doesn't this unfortunate woman look at herself in the mirror? Doesn't she see the ravages of years of hard work? These village people attribute everything to potions or jealousies. . . . For instance, they don't find work. . . . Jealousy is to blame. . . . Some scheme doesn't come out right. . . . Jealousy. The person who attributes all his disasters to the envy of others is in reality an envious person. Aren't we all? Haven't I perhaps been given a potion?"

During the next few days he was obsessed with the idea of a philter, a potion. At length he said to himself: "That is the original sin!"

CHAPTER 9

Joaquín married Antonia in his search for shelter; the poor woman guessed at her mission from the first, the role she was to play in her husband's heart, as a shield and a source of consolation. She was taking a sick man for a husband, a man who was perhaps an incurable spiritual invalid; her duty would be that of a nurse. And she accepted her destiny with a heart full of compassion, full of love for the misfortune of the person who was joining his life with hers.

Antonia felt that between her and her Joaquín there was an invisible wall, a crystalline and transparent wall of ice. That man could not belong to his wife, for he did not belong to himself, he was not master of himself, but was, instead, both alienated and possessed. Even in the most intimate transports of conjugal relations, an invisible shadow of prophetic melancholy fell between them. Her husband's kisses seemed to her stolen kisses, when they were not the kisses of madness.

Joaquín avoided speaking of his cousin Helena in front of his wife, and Antonia, who noticed this self-conscious avoidance at once, did not fail to bring her into the conversation at every turn.

This was at the beginning, for a little later she avoided mentioning her any more.

One day Joaquín was called to Abel's house in his capacity of doctor. There he learned that Helena was already bearing the fruit of her marriage to Abel, while Antonia showed no signs of such fruition. The unhappy doctor was assaulted by a shameful suggestion which arose to humiliate him; some devil was taunting him: "Do you only see? He is even more of a man than you are! He, who through his art resurrects and immortalizes those you allow to die because of your dullness, he is to have a child, he is to bring into the world a new being, a work of his own, created in flesh, and blood, and bone, while you . . . You probably are not even capable of . . . He is more of a man than you!"

He arrived at the shelter of his own home downcast and brooding.

"Have you come from Abel's house?" his wife asked.

"Yes. How did you happen to know?"

"It's in your face. That house is your torment. You should not go there. . . ."

"And what should I do?"

"Excuse yourself from going! Your health and peace of mind come first. . . ."

"These are only apprehensions of yours. . . ."

"No, Joaquín, don't try to conceal it from

me . . ."—and she was unable to continue, the tears drowning her voice.

The unfortunate Antonia sank to the ground. Her sobs seemed torn from her body by the roots.

"What is the matter, woman, what is all this? . . ."

"Only tell me, Joaquín, what afflicts you. Confide in me, confess yourself to me. . . ."

"I have nothing to accuse myself for . . ."

"Come, will you tell me the truth, Joaquín, the truth?"

For a moment, he hesitated, seeming to struggle with an invisible enemy, with his Guardian Devil, and then, his voice animated with a sudden, desperate resolution, he almost cried out:

"Yes, I will tell you the truth, the entire truth!"

"You love Helena. You're still in love with Helena."

"No, I am not! I am not! I was, but I am no longer."

"Well then? . . ."

"Then what?"

"What is this torture in which you live? Why is that house, Helena's house, the source of your misery? That house does not let you live in peace. It's Helena. . . ."

"Helena, no! It's Abel!"

"Are you jealous of Abel?"

"Yes, I am jealous of him! I hate him, I hate him, I hate him"—and Joaquín made his hands into fists as he spoke through clenched teeth.

"If you are jealous of Abel . . . then you must love Helena."

"No, I don't love her. If she belonged to someone else, I should not be jealous of that person. No, I don't love Helena. I despise her, I despise that peacock of a woman, that professional beauty, the fashionable painter's model, Abel's mistress. . . ."

"For God's sake, Joaquín, for God's sake! . . ."

"Yes, his mistress . . . his legitimized mistress. Do you think that the benediction of a priest changes an affair into a marriage?"

"Listen, Joaquín, we're married just as they are. . . ."

"As they are, not at all, Antonia, not at all! They got married only to demean me, to humiliate and denigrate me; they married to mock me; they married to hurt me."

The poor man burst into sobs which choked him, cutting off his breathing. He seemed to die.

"Antonia . . . Antonia . . ." he whispered in a little smothered voice.

"My poor child!" she exclaimed, embracing him.

She reached up and took his head in her lap

as if he were a sick child, caressing him while she said:

"Calm yourself, my Joaquín, calm yourself . . . I am here, your wife is here, all yours and only yours. And now that I know all your secrets, I am yours more than before and I love you more than ever. . . . Forget them . . . scorn them. . . . It would have been all the worse if such a woman had loved you."

"Yes, but it's he, Antonia, it's he. . . ."

"Forget him!"

"I cannot forget him. . . . He pursues me. . . . His fame, his renown follow me everywhere. . . ."

"If you work, you will have fame and renown, for you are not any less than he. Leave your practice, we don't need it. We can go to Renada, to the house which belonged to my parents, and there you can devote yourself to what you like best, to science, to making discoveries of the sort that will earn you notice. . . . I will help you in every way I can. . . . I will see that you are not distracted . . . and you will be more than he. . . ."

"I cannot, Antonia, I cannot. His successes take away my sleep and would not allow me to work in peace. . . . The vision of his awesome paintings would come between my eye and the microscope and would prevent my seeing anything others have not seen. . . . I cannot. . . . I cannot. . . .

Then, lowering his voice like a child, stammering almost, as if stunned by his fall into the abyss of humiliation, he sobbed:

"And they are going to have a child, Antonia. . . ."

"We will have one also," she whispered in his ear, covering it with a kiss; "the Holy Virgin will not deny me, for I ask her every day. . . . Or the holy water of Lourdes . . ."

"Do you, too, believe in potions, Antonia?"

"I believe in God!"

" 'I believe in God,' " Joaquín repeated when he was alone—alone with the other presence, with his obsession. "What does it mean, to believe in God? Where is God? I shall have to find Him!"

CHAPTER 10

When Abel had his child—Joaquín wrote in his *Confession*—*I felt hate fester in me. He had invited me to attend Helena in her labor, but I had excused myself by saying that I did not attend deliveries, which was true, and that I would not be able to maintain my sangfroid, the necessary cold-bloodedness—benumbed-bloodedness, I should have said—where my cousin was concerned, should she fall into danger. And yet, my own devil suggested the ferocious temptation: attend her and smother the child surreptitiously. I was able to overcome myself and suppress this revolting thought.*

This new triumph of Abel's, of Abel the man and not the artist only—for the child was a beauty, a masterpiece of health and vigor, a little angel, as everyone said—bound me all the more to Antonia, from whom I was expecting a child of my own. I longed to make of my wife, I needed to make of this poor victim of my blind rage—the real victim even more than I was myself—I needed to make of her, to make her be, the mother of my children, flesh of my flesh, heart of my heart, entrails of my entrails which were tortured by the devil. She would be the mother of my children and for that reason su-

perior to the mothers of the children of others. She, unhappy woman, had chosen me, the antipathetic, the despised, the affronted one; she had taken up what another woman had refused with disdain and scorn. And she even spoke well of them to me!

Abel's child, little Abelin—for they gave it the same name as the father, as if to continue his lineage and fame—the young Abel, who would with the passage of time be the instrument of my revenge, was a marvel of a child. I needed to have one like him, but even more beautiful.

CHAPTER 11

"What are you working on these days?" Joaquín asked Abel one day. The doctor had come to Abel's house to see the child, and had afterwards gone on to visit the painter in his study.

"Well, next I shall paint a historical piece, actually a scene from the Old Testament; at the moment, I am doing research for it. . . ."

"How is that? Looking for models from that epoch?"

"No; reading the Bible and commentaries on it."

"I am well advised when I say that you are a scientific painter. . . ."

"And you, an artistic doctor, isn't that so?"

"Worse than a scientific artist, you're a literary one! Beware of making literature with your brush!"

"Thanks for the advice."

"And what will the subject of your painting be?"

"The death of Abel at the hands of Cain, the first fratricide."

Joaquín turned whiter than ever; gazing fixedly at his first friend he asked in a half-suppressed voice:

"How did you happen to think of that?"

"Very simply," Abel answered without perceiving his friend's meaning; "it was the suggestiveness of the name. Since my name is Abel. . . . I had made two nude studies. . . ."

"Nude of body. . . ."

"Even of soul. . . ."

"You mean to paint their souls?"

"Of course! The soul of Cain, the soul of envy. And the soul of Abel. . . ."

"What is he the soul of?"

"I wish I knew. I'm trying to find out, but I can't put my finger on the right expression. I want to paint him before his death, thrown to the ground and fatally wounded by his brother. I've got *Genesis* here, and I'm reading Lord Byron's *Cain;* do you know the book?"

"Byron's *Cain* I don't know. What have you gotten from the Bible?"

"Very little. . . . You'll see," and, taking up the book, he read: "'And Adam knew Eve his wife: who conceived and brought forth Cain, saying: I have gotten a man through God. And again she brought forth his brother Abel. And Abel was a shepherd, and Cain a husbandman. And it came to pass after many days, that Cain offered, of the fruits of the earth, gifts to the Lord. Abel also offered of the firstlings of his flock, and of their fat: and the Lord had respect to Abel, and to his offerings. But to Cain and his offerings he had no respect. . . .' "

"And why was that?" interrupted Joaquín. "Why did God look with respect on the offering of Abel and look with disfavor on Cain and his offering? . . ."

"It isn't explained here. . . ."

"And haven't you asked yourself the question before setting out to paint your picture?"

"Not yet. . . . Perhaps because God already saw in Cain the future killer of his brother, the invidious. . . ."

"If he was invidious it was because God had made him invidious, and had given him a philter. Go on with the reading."

" 'And Cain was exceedingly angry, and his countenance fell. And the Lord said to him: Why art thou angry? And why is thy countenance fallen? If thou do well, shall thou not receive? But if ill, shall not sin forthwith be present at the door? But the lust thereof shall be under thee, and thou shalt have dominion over it. . . .' "

"Instead, sin dominated him," interrupted Joaquín again, "because God had abandoned him. Go on."

" 'And Cain said to Abel his brother: Let us go forth abroad. And when they were in the field, Cain rose up against his brother Abel, and slew him. And the Lord said to Cain. . . .' "

"That's enough! Don't read any more. I'm not interested in what Jehovah told Cain after there was no help for the matter."

Joaquín rested his elbows on the table, his face between the palms of his hands. He fixed a sharp, frozen stare on Abel, who became alarmed at he knew not what. And then Joaquín said:

"Have you ever heard of the joke they play on children who learn Sacred History?"

"No."

"Well, they ask them, 'Who killed Cain?'; and the children, completely confused, answer: 'His brother Abel.' "

"I never heard that."

"You have heard it now. And tell me, since you are going to paint this Biblical scene—and how like the Bible it is!—hasn't it occurred to you that if Cain had not killed Abel, it would have been Abel who would have ended by killing Cain?"

"How can you think of such a thing?"

"Abel's sheep were acceptable to God, and Abel the shepherd found grace in the eyes of the Lord, but neither the fruits of the earth offered up by Cain, the husbandman, nor Cain himself found favor with God. His favorite was Abel. The God-forsaken was Cain. . . ."

"And what fault was that of Abel's?"

"Ah, you think, do you, that the fortunate, the favored, are not to blame? The truth is that they are to blame for not concealing—and not concealing it as a shameful thing, which it is—every gratuitous favor, every privilege not earned on proper merit; for not concealing this grace instead of making an ostentatious show of it. For I have no doubt but that Abel flaunted his favor under the snouts of Cain's beasts, or that he taunted him with the smoke of the sheep he offered to God. Those who believe themselves to be of the company of the just tend to be supremely arrogant people bent on crushing others under the ostentation of their 'justice.' As someone once said, there is no worse canaille than 'honorable' people. . . ."

"And are you sure," asked the painter, who had become apprehensive over the serious aspect the conversation had assumed, "are you sure that Abel boasted of his good fortune?"

"I have no doubt of it, or of the fact that he showed no respect for his elder brother; I do not suppose, either, that he asked the Lord to show his elder brother some favor too. And I know something else; and that is that Abel's successors, the Abelites, have invented Hell as a place for the Cainites, because, if there were no such place, the Abelites would find all their glory insipid. Their pleasure is to see others suffer while they themselves stay free of suffering."

"Joaquín, Joaquín, how very sick you are!"

"You're right. And no one can doctor themselves. . . . Let me have this *Cain* of Lord Byron's, I want to read it."

"Take it."

"And tell me, doesn't your wife supply you with any inspiration for this painting? Doesn't she provide you with any ideas?"

"My wife? . . . There was no woman in this tragedy."

"There is in every tragedy, Abel."

"Perhaps Eve. . . ."

"Perhaps. . . . Perhaps the woman who gave them both the same milk; or potion. . . ."

CHAPTER 12

Joaquín read Lord Byron's *Cain*. And later he wrote in his *Confession:*

The effect made upon me by reading that book was dreadful. I felt the need to give vent to my feelings, and so I took some notes, which I still have and which are now here before me. And I wonder now if I took them down merely to unburden myself? No, I undoubtedly thought to make use of them some day in writing a great book. Vanity consumes us. We make a spectacle of our most intimate and vile disabilities. I can imagine the existence of a man who would want to have a pestiferous tumor such as no one has ever had before, solely in order to vaunt it about, and to call attention to the struggle he was waging against it. This very Confession, *for instance, isn't it something more than a mere unburdening of soul?*

I have sometimes thought of tearing it up, so as to free myself from it. But would that free me? No! It is better to make a spectacle than to consume oneself. After all is said and done, life itself is no more than a spectacle.

The reading of Byron's Cain *penetrated me to the core. How right Cain was to blame his parents for having taken the fruits of the tree of science instead of those of the tree of life! For me, at any rate, science has not done more than exacerbate the wound.*

Would that I had never lived! *I say with Cain. Why was I created? Why must I live? What I do not understand is why Cain did not choose suicide. That would have been the most noble beginning for the human race. But then, why didn't Adam and Eve kill themselves after the fall and before they gave birth to children? Ah, perhaps because Jehovah would have created other such beings as they, another Cain and another Abel? Isn't this same tragedy perhaps repeated in other worlds, up there among the stars?*

Perhaps the tragedy has been performed elsewhere, the first-night performance on earth not having quite sufficed. Was it opening night, after all?

When I read how Lucifer declared to Cain that he, Cain, was immortal, at that moment I began to wonder fearfully if I, too, and my hatred with me, were immortal. Must I have a soul; *I asked myself,* is my hatred the soul? *And I came to think finally that it could not be otherwise, that such a hatred could not be the property of the body. That which I could not find in others with a scalpel I now found in myself. A corruptible organism could not hate as I did. Lucifer had aspired to be God, and I, ever since*

I was very young, had I not aspired to reduce everyone else to nothing? But how could I have been so unfortunate, unless I was made that way by the creator of all misfortune?

It required no effort for Abel to take care of his sheep, just as it required no effort for the other Abel to paint his pictures; for me, on the contrary, a very great effort was needed to diagnose the ills of my patients.

Cain complained that Adah, his own beloved Adah, his wife and his sister, did not understand the mind which overwhelmed him. But my Adah, my poor Adah understood my mind well enough. In all truth, she was a Christian. But then, I did not, in the end, find any sympathy either.

Until I read and re-read the Byronic Cain, *I, who had seen so many men die, had not thought of death, had not* discovered *it. I began to wonder if I would die with my hate, if my hate would die with me, or outlast me; I wondered if hate outlived the haters, if it were something material, transmissible; I speculated as to whether hatred were not the soul, the quintessence of the soul. And I began to believe in Hell, and in Death as a being, as the Devil, as hatred made flesh, as the God of the soul. Everything that science did not explain, the terrible poem of that great hater Lord Byron made clear to me.*

My Adah, too, would taunt me gently when I did not work, when I could not work. And

Lucifer stood between my Adah and myself. Walk not with this spirit! *my Adah cried. Poor Antonia! And she begged me to save her too from the spirit. My poor Adah did not go so far as to hate these influences as much as I did. But then, did I go so far as truly to love my Antonia? Ah, if only I had been capable of loving her I would have been saved. She was for me another instrument of my vengeance. I wanted her as the mother of a son or a daughter who would revenge me. Although I did think, quite naïvely, that once I became a father, I would be cured of all this. Still, hadn't I gotten married simply to produce hateful beings like myself, to transmit my hatred, to immortalize it?*

The scene between Cain and Lucifer in the Abyss of Space remained engraved in my soul as if it had been burned in. I saw my science in the light of my sin and the wretchedness of giving life in order to propagate death. And I saw clearly that this immortal hatred constituted my soul. This hatred, I thought, must have preceded my birth and would survive after my death. I was shaken with horror to think of living always so as to abhor always. This was Hell. And I had so scoffed at belief in ıt! It was a literal Hell!

When I read how Aaah spoke to Cain of his son, of Enoch, I thought of the son, or the daughter I would surely have; I thought of you, my daughter, my redemption and my consola-

tion; I thought of how you would come one day to save me. And as I read of what Cain said to his own sleeping, innocent son, who knew not that he was naked, *I wondered if it had not been a crime in me to have engendered you, my poor daughter! Do you forgive me for having created you? As I read what Adah said to her Cain, I remembered my own years in paradise, when I was not yet on the hunt for rewards, when I did not dream of surpassing all the others. No, my daughter, no; I did not offer up my studies to God with a pure heart; I did not seek truth and knowledge, but instead sought prizes, and fame, and the chance to be more than he was.*

He, Abel, loved his art and cultivated it with a purity of purpose, and never strove to impose on me. No, it was not he who took away my peace. And yet I had gone so far, demented as I was, as to think of overturning Abel's altar! The truth was I had thought only of myself.

The narrative of Abel's death as it is given us by that terrible poet of the Devil blinded me. As I read I felt everything grow dark, and I think I suffered a fainting spell, and a kind of nausea. And from that day on, thanks to the impious Byron, I began to believe.

CHAPTER 13

Antonia presented Joaquín with a daughter. "A daughter," he told himself; "and *he* has a son!" But he soon recovered from this new trick of his demon. And he began to love his daughter with all the force of his passion, and through her, her mother as well. "She shall be my avenger," he said to himself at first, without knowing what it was she was to avenge him for; but later: "She shall be my salvation, my purification."

I began to keep this record, he wrote in the *Confession, a little later, for my daughter's sake, so that once I was dead, she might know her poor father, and feel for him, and love him. As I watched her sleeping in her cradle, innocently dreaming, I thought how in order to bring her up and educate her in purity I should have to purify myself of my passion, cleanse myself of the leprosy of my soul. And I decided to make certain she should love, love everyone, and love* them *in particular. There, upon the innocence of her dreams, I swore to free myself from my infernal chains. I vowed to be the chief herald of Abel's greatness.*

Abel Sanchez completed his historical canvas

and entered it in a large exhibition. There it received widespread acclaim and was hailed as a true masterpiece; inevitably, he was awarded the medal of honor.

Joaquín went often to the exhibition hall to view the painting and to look into it, as into a looking-glass, at the painted Cain, and to watch then the eyes of the people, to see if they looked at him after looking at the other figure.

I was tortured by the suspicion, he wrote in the *Confession, that Abel had thought of me when he was painting his Cain, that he had sounded all the depths in the conversation we had held at his house at the time he first told me of his intention to paint his subject and when he had read the passages from* Genesis—*when I had so completely forgotten him and so completely bared my sickened soul as I thought only of myself. But no, there was not in Abel's Cain the least resemblance to me; he had not thought of me in the painting; he had not attempted to attack me, to denigrate me, nor had Helena apparently influenced him against me. It sufficed them to savor the future triumph, the triumph they were anticipating. They did not even think of me now!*

And this idea that they did not even think of me, did not even hate me, tortured me more than the other idea had. To be hated by him, *with a hatred such as mine for him, would have been something after all, and could have been my salvation.*

And so Joaquín surpassed himself, or simply plumbed himself deeper, and conceived the idea of giving a banquet to celebrate Abel's triumph. He, Joaquín, Abel's everlasting friend, his "friend from before they knew each other," would arrange a banquet for the painter.

Joaquín had a certain fame as an orator. At the Academy of Medicine and Sciences it was he who overawed the others with his cold and cutting manner of address, usually over-precise and sarcastic. His speeches had the effect of a stream of cold water poured upon the enthusiasms of the newcomers; they were dour lessons in pessimistic skepticism. His usual thesis was that nothing was known for certain in medicine, that everything was hypothetical and a constant raveling and unraveling, that distrust was the most justified emotion. For these reasons, when it became known that it was Joaquín who was giving the banquet, most people joyously made ready for an inevitably double-edged address, a pitiless dissection—in the guise of a panegyric—on the subject of scientific, documentary painting; at best, it would be a sarcastic encomium. A malevolent anticipation titillated the hearts of all those who had ever heard Joaquín speak of

Abel's painting. And they warned the latter of his peril.

"You are mistaken," Abel told them. "I know Joaquín and do not believe him capable of such a thing. I know something of what is going on within him, but he is possessed of a profound artistic sense, and whatever he says will probably be well worth hearing. I should like next to paint a portrait of him."

"A portrait?"

"Yes, you don't know him as I do. His is a fiery, turbulent soul."

"A colder man. . . ."

"On the outside. In any case, fire burns, as they say. For my purposes, he couldn't be better, a face made on purpose. . . ."

This opinion of Abel's reached the ears of his subject, who once more sank into the sea of speculation. "What must he really think of me?" he asked himself. "Does he really think me to be a 'fiery, turbulent soul'? Or does he in reality see that I am a victim of a whim of fate?"

At this time he went so far as to do something for which he was later deeply ashamed. It happened that a maid entered his service who had formerly served in Abel's house, and he made overtures to her, confidentially importuning her—without compromising himself—for the sole purpose of ascertaining what she might have heard about him in the other house.

"Come now, is it possible you never heard them speak of me?"

"They said nothing, sir, absolutely nothing."

"Didn't they ever speak of me?"

"Well, talk they did, just talk; but they said nothing."

"Nothing, never anything?"

"I didn't hear them speak very much. At table, while I served them, they spoke very little, and only of those small things usually spoken of at the table. About his paintings. . . ."

"I understand. But nothing, never anything about me?"

"I don't remember anything."

As he left the maid he was seized with a profound self-aversion. "I'm making an idiot of myself," he said to himself. "What must this girl think of me!" He was so humiliated by his action that he contrived the girl's dismissal on some small pretext. "But suppose she goes back now into Abel's service," he asked himself then, "and tells him all this?" So that he was on the point of asking his wife to summon her back. But he dared not. And thereafter he shuddered at the thought of meeting her in the street.

CHAPTER 14

The day of the banquet arrived. Joaquín had not slept on the night before.

"I am going to the battle, Antonia," he told his wife as he left the house.

"May God light your way and guide you, Joaquín."

"I should like to see the little girl, our poor little Joaquinita. . . ."

"Yes, come and see her . . . she's sleeping. . . ."

"Poor little thing! She doesn't yet know the Devil exists! But I swear to you, Antonia, I shall learn to tear him from me. I will tear him out, I will strangle him, and I will throw him at the feet of Abel. . . . I would give her a kiss if I weren't afraid of waking her. . . ."

"No, no! Kiss her!"

The father bent over and kissed the sleeping child, who smiled in her dreams as she felt herself kissed.

"You see, Joaquín, she blesses you too."

"Goodbye, my wife!" And he kissed her, with a very long kiss.

Antonia was left behind to pray before the statue of the Virgin Mary.

A malicious undercurrent of expectation ran through the conversation at the banquet table.

Joaquín, seated on Abel's right, was very pale; he scarcely ate or spoke. Abel himself began to feel some trepidation.

As the dessert was served, some of the diners began to hiss as a call for silence, and a hush fell, in which someone said: "Let him speak." Joaquín stood up. He began to talk in a muffled, trembling voice; but soon it cleared and began to vibrate with a new accent. His voice filled the silence, and nothing else was to be heard. The surprise was general. A more ardent, more impassioned eulogy had scarcely ever been heard, or one more filled with admiration and affection for both the artist and his work. Many felt tears springing to their eyes as Joaquín evoked the days of his common infancy with Abel, when neither of them yet dreamed of what they would one day become.

"No one has known him more intimately than I," he said; "I believe I know you," addressing Abel, "better than I know myself, with more purity, because looking into one's own heart one tends to see only the dust from which one has been created. It is in others that we see the best part of ourselves, a part which we can love; and thus, our admiration. He has accomplished in his art what I should like to have accomplished in mine; for this reason, he is one of my models; his glory is a spur to my work and is a consolation for the glory which I have not been able to gain. He belongs to us all; above all he is mine, and I, enriched by his work, try to make this work as much mine as he made it his by the act of creation. Thus am I able to be a satisfied subject of my mediocrity. . . ."

From time to time his voice cried out. His audience was under his spell, obscurely aware of the titanic battle between this soul and its demon.

"And behold the face of Cain"—Joaquín let the fiery words form like single drops—"the tragic Cain, the roving husbandman, the first to found cities, the father of industry, envy and community life. Behold his face! See with what affection, with what compassion, with what love the unfortunate is painted. Wretched Cain! Our Abel Sanchez *admires* Cain just as Milton admired Satan, he is enamored of his Cain just as Milton was of his Satan, for to admire is to love and to love is to pity. Our Abel has sensed all the misery, all the unmerited misfortune of the one who killed the first Abel, and who, according to Biblical legend, brought death into the world. Our Abel makes us understand Cain's guilt, for guilt there was, and he makes us pity him and love him. . . . This painting is an act of love!"

When Joaquín finished speaking, there was a heavy silence, until a salvo of applause thundered out. Abel stood up then; pale, shaking, hesitatingly, with tears in his eyes, he addressed his friend:

"What you have said, Joaquín, is worth more,

has greater value, much greater, than my painting, than all the paintings I have made, than those that I shall ever make. . . . Your words are a work of art, and of the heart. I did not know what I had accomplished until I heard you. You, and not I, have made my painting, you alone!"

The two eternal friends embraced amid their own tears and the clamorous applause and cheers of the assemblage, which had risen to its feet.

In the middle of the embrace his demon whispered to Joaquín: "If you could only crush him in your arms! . . ."

"Stupendous," they were saying. "What an orator! What a great speech! Who would have thought . . . ? It's a shame that there were no reporters present!"

"Prodigious!" said one man, "I don't expect to hear another such speech again."

"Chills ran through me as I listened," said another.

"Just see how pale he is!"

Such was the case, in truth. Joaquín, as he resumed his seat following his success, felt overcome, overborne by a wave of sadness. No, his demon was not yet dead. His address had been a success the like of which he had never before enjoyed, nor would likely enjoy again, and now the idea came to him of devoting himself to speaking as a means of gaining a fame which would obscure the fame of his friend in painting.

"Did you see how Abel wept?" one man asked as he came out.

"The truth is that this address by Joaquín is worth all the paintings of the other. The speech made the painting. It will be necessary to call it The Painting of the Speech. Take away the speech, and what's left of the painting! Nothing, despite the first prize."

When Joaquín arrived home, Antonia came out to open the door and to embrace him:

"I already know, they've already told me. Yes, yes! You're better than he, much better. He must know that if his painting is to have value it will be because of your speech."

"It's true, Antonia, it's true, but . . ."

"But what? Do you still . . ."

"Still! I don't wish to tell you the things my demon whispered while Abel and I embraced. . . ."

"No, don't tell me!"

She closed his mouth with a long, warm, humid kiss, as her eyes grew moist with tears.

"Let's see if you can draw the demon out of me this way, Antonia; let's see if you can suck him out."

"Should I absorb him then, so that he stays in me?" the poor woman asked, trying to laugh.

"Yes, draw him in, for he can't harm you; in you he will die, he will drown in your blood as in holy water. . . ."

At his home, Abel found himself alone with Helena. She said:

"I've been told all about Joaquín's oration. He's had to swallow your triumph . . . he's had to swallow it! . . ."

"Don't talk that way; you didn't hear him."

"It's just as if I had."

"His words came from the heart. I was deeply moved. I must tell you that even I did not know what I had painted until I heard his exposition."

"Don't trust him . . . don't trust him . . . when he eulogizes you like that, it must be for some reason. . . ."

"Might he not have said what he felt?"

"You know he is dying with envy of you. . . ."

"Be quiet!"

"Dying, yes, almost dead, with envy of you. . . ."

"Be quiet, woman, be quiet!"

"No; and it's not jealousy, for he no longer loves me, if he ever did . . . it's envy . . . envy. . . ."

"Be quiet!" roared Abel.

"All right, I'll be quiet, but you shall see. . . ."

"I've already seen and heard, and that's enough. Be quiet, now!"

CHAPTER 15

And yet, that heroic act did not restore poor Joaquín.

I began to feel remorse, he wrote in his *Confession, of having said what I had, of not having let my evil passion pour forth and thus gotten free of it, of not having broken with him artistically, denouncing the falsity and affectation of his art, his imitation, his cold, calculated technique, his lack of emotion. I was sorry for not having destroyed his fame. By so doing I would have freed myself, told the truth, and reduced his prestige to its true scale. Who knows but that Cain, the Biblical Cain, who killed the other Abel, began to love his victim as soon as he saw him dead. And it was at this juncture that I began really to believe: among the effects of that address were the elements of my conversion.*

The conversion alluded to by Joaquín in his *Confession* proceeded from the fact that his wife Antonia, seeing her husband was not cured—fearing that he was perhaps incurable—induced him to seek help in prayer, and in the religion of his fathers, the religion which was hers, the religion which would be their daughter's.

"You should first go to Confession."

"But I haven't been to church for years."

"All the same. . . ."

"But I don't believe in these things. . . ."

"You believe you don't. But the priest has explained to me how it is that you men of science believe you don't believe, and all the same believe. I know that the things your mother taught you, the things I shall teach our daughter . . ."

"All right, all right, leave me alone!"

"No, I will not. Go and confess yourself, I beg you."

"And what will the people who know my ideas say?"

"Oh, is that it? Is it out of social considerations. . . ."

However, Joaquín's heart was touched, and he asked himself if he really did not believe; moreover, he wanted to see if the Church could cure him, even if he did not believe. And he began to frequent the services, almost too conspicuously, as if by way of challenge to those who knew his irreligious convictions; finally, he sought out a confessor. And, once in the confessional, his soul was loosed.

"I hate him, Father, I hate him with all my heart, and if I did not believe as I do, or as I want to believe, I would kill him. . . ."

"But that, my son, that is not necessarily hatred. It is more like envy."

"All hatred is envy, Father, all hatred is envy."

"You should change it into noble emulation, into a desire to succeed in your profession, and in the service of God, to do the best you can accomplish. . . ."

"I cannot, I cannot, I cannot work. His fame and glory do not allow me."

"You must make an effort . . . it is for this purpose that man is free. . . ."

"I do not believe in free will, Father. I am a doctor."

"Still . . ."

"What did I do that God should make me this way, rancorous, envious, evil? What bad blood did my father bequeath me?"

"My son . . . my son. . . ."

"No, I do not believe in human liberty, and whoever cannot believe in liberty is surely not free. And I am not! To be free is to believe oneself free!"

"It is evil of one to doubt God."

"Is it evil to doubt, Father?"

"I don't mean to say that, but simply that your evil passion comes from your doubting God. . . ."

"Is it evil, then, to doubt God? I ask you again."

"Yes, it is evil."

"Then I doubt God because he made me evil. Just as he made Cain evil, God made me doubt. . . ."

"He made you free."

Miguel de Unamuno

"Yes, free to be evil."
"And to be good!"
"Ah, why was I born, Father?"
"Ask rather to what end. . . ."

CHAPTER 16

Abel had painted a Virgin with the Child in arms: the painting was in actuality a portrait of Helena, and the child, Abelito. It had been well received, was reproduced and, before a splendid photograph of it, Joaquín prayed the most holy Virgin, asking her to protect and save him.

But while he prayed, susurrating in a low voice, as if to hear himself, he fought to stifle another voice more profound, which welled from deep within him saying: "If he would only die! If he would only leave her free for you!"

"So," Abel hailed him one day, "you have become a reactionary."

"I have?"

"Yes, they tell me you have given yourself up to the church and go to Mass every day. Since you never did believe either in God or the Devil, —and it can scarcely be a matter of having made a conversion just like that—well, then, you must have turned reactionary!"

"What does it all matter to you?"

"I'm not calling you to account, you understand. But, well now . . . do you really believe?"

"I need to believe."

"That's something else again. I mean do you really believe?"

"As I've already told you, I need to believe. Don't ask me again."

"For my part, art is enough. Art is my religion."

"Still, you have painted Virgins. . . ."

"Yes, Helena."

"Who is not precisely a virgin. . . ."

"For me, it's as if she were. She is the mother of my child. . . ."

"Only that?"

"And every mother is a virgin by virtue of being a mother."

"You're entering the realms of theology!"

"I don't know about that, but I hate stupid conservatism and prudery, which is something born merely of envy, it seems to me, and it surprises me to find signs of it in you. I had faith in your being able to withstand the mediocrity of the vulgar, and I am surprised to see you wearing their uniform."

"What do you mean, Abel? Come, explain yourself."

"It's clear enough. Common, vulgar spirits are never distinguished, and, unable to bear the fact that others are, they attempt to impose upon others more fortunate the uniform of dogma—which is a kind of dull fatigue uniform—so that the uncommon may appear undistinguished. The origin of all orthodoxy, in religion as in art, is envy, have no doubt of it. If we were all to dress as we pleased, there would be one among us who would think up some striking mode of dress which would accentuate his natural elegance; if it were a man who did this, women would naturally be attracted to him; and yet if a vulgar, common individual were to do the same thing, he would merely look ridiculous. It is for this reason that the vulgar, that is to say, the envious, have invented a kind of uniform, a manner of dressing themselves like puppets, which comes to be the fashion—for fashion, too, is another matter of orthodoxy. Don't deceive yourself, Joaquín, those ideas which are called dangerous, daring, impious, are merely those that never suggest themselves to the poor routine intelligences, the people who don't have even a grain of personal initiative or originality, but do have 'common sense'—and vulgarity. Imagination is what they most hate—especially since the fact is that they don't have any."

"Even though this is the case," Joaquín exclaimed, "don't those we call the vulgar, the common, the mediocre have the right to defend themselves?"

"On another occasion, at my house, you remember, you defended Cain, the envious; then, later, in that unforgettable speech which I shall repeat till I die, in that speech—to which I owe a good deal of my reputation—you showed us, at least you showed me, Cain's soul. But Cain was scarcely a mediocrity, a vulgarian, a common man. . . ."

"But he was the father of all the envious."

"Yes, but of another kind of envy, not the envy of the bigots. . . . Cain's envy was something grandiose; the envy of the fanatical inquisitor is picayune and miserably small. And it shocks me to see you on the side of the inquisitors."

"Can this man read my thoughts, then?" Joaquín asked himself as he took leave of Abel. "He doesn't seem to notice what I suffer, and still . . . He talks and thinks in the same way he paints, without knowing what he says or paints. He works unconsciously, no matter how much I try to see in him the thoughtful technician. . . ."

CHAPTER 17

Joaquín became aware that Abel was involved with one of his former models; this information corroborated his suspicion that Abel had not married Helena from motives of love. "They married," Joaquín told himself, "to humiliate me." And he added: "And Helena doesn't love him, nor is she capable of loving him . . . she doesn't love anyone, she's incapable of affection; she's no more than a beautiful shell of vanity. . . . She married from vanity and disdain for me, and from vanity or caprice she is capable of betraying her husband . . . even with the man she didn't want as husband." A spark glowed among the embers of recollections, a live coal which he had thought extinguished under his ice-cold hatred: it was his old love for Helena. Yes, in spite of everything he was still enamored of this female peacock, this coquette, this artist's model to her husband. Antonia was very much superior to her, without any doubt, but the other was the other. Then, there was revenge . . . and revenge was so sweet! So warming to a frozen heart!

In a few days he went to Abel's house, carefully choosing an hour when Abel himself would be out. He found his cousin Helena alone with her child, Helena before whose image made divine he had vainly sought protection and salvation.

"Abel has told me," Helena said to him now, "that you've taken up going to church. Is it because Antonia has dragged you there, or do you go there to escape Antonia?"

"What do you mean?"

"You husbands tend to become holy men either while tracking down a wife, or escaping her. . . ."

"There are those who escape their wives, but not precisely to go to church."

"Oh?"

"Yes. But your husband, who has borne this tale to you, doesn't seem to know something else, which is that the church is not the only place where I pray. . . ."

"Naturally not! Every devout man should say prayers at home."

"And I do. And my chief prayer is to the Virgin, to ask her for protection and salvation."

"That strikes me as very sensible."

"And do you know before whose image I ask this?"

"Not unless you are to tell me. . . ."

"Before the painting made by your husband. . . ."

Helena turned away abruptly, her face deeply flushed, toward the child sleeping in a corner of the parlor. The suddenness of the attack had disconcerted her. Composing herself, however, she said:

"This is an act of impiety on your part, Joaquín, and proves that your new devotion is no more than a farce, and perhaps something worse. . . ."

"I swear to you, Helena. . . ."

"The second commandment—don't take His holy name in vain."

"Therefore I truly swear to you, Helena, that my conversion was sincere; I mean that I have wanted to believe, I have wanted to defend myself with faith against a passion that devours me. . . ."

"Yes, I know your passion. . . ."

"No, you don't know it!"

"*I know it.* It is that you cannot endure Abel's existence."

"Why can't I endure him?"

"That is something only you may know. You have never been able to endure him, not even before you introduced him to me."

"That's untrue, utterly untrue!"

"It's the truth! The utter truth!"

"Why should I not be able to endure him?"

"Because he is becoming well known, because he has a reputation. . . . Don't you have a good practice? Don't you make a good living?"

"Listen, Helena, I am going to tell you the

truth, all of it! I am not satisfied with what I have. I wanted to become famous, to find something new in my science, to link my name to some scientific discovery. . . ."

"Well, then, apply yourself to it, for it's not talent you lack."

"Apply myself . . . apply myself. . . . Yes, I could have applied myself, Helena, if I had been able to offer up the triumph at your feet. . . ."

"And why not at Antonia's feet?"

"Please, let's not speak of her."

"Ah, have you come for this, then! Have you waited until my Abel"—and she emphasized the *my*—"was gone, so that you could come for this?"

"Your Abel . . . your Abel . . . a precious lot of attention your Abel is paying you!"

"Oh? Do you also play the role of informer, tattletale, gossip?"

"Your Abel has other models beside you."

"What of it?" Helena exclaimed, bridling. "And what if he does have them? It's a sign that he knows how to win them! Or, are you jealous of him for that too? Is it because you haven't any recourse but to content yourself with . . . your Antonia? Ah, and because he has shown that he knew how to find himself another, have you thought of coming here today to find yourself another too? And do you come to me like this, to bring me these tales? Aren't you ashamed?

Get away from me, get out! The sight of you makes me sick."

"O my God! Stop, Helena, you're killing me . . . you're killing me!"

"Go, go to church, you hypocrite, you envious hypocrite; go and let your wife take care of you and cure you, for you are very sick."

"Helena, Helena, only you can cure me! In the name of all you love most, remember you are condemning a man and losing him forever!"

"Ah, and in order to save you, you would have me lose another man, my own?"

"You won't lose him; you've already lost him. He's not interested in any part of you. He's incapable of loving you. I, I am the one who loves you, with all my soul, with a love that you can't conceive."

Helena stood up, went over to the child and, awakening him, took him in her arms; then she turned around to Joaquín and said: "Get out! This child, the son of Abel, orders you from his house. Get out!"

CHAPTER 18

Joaquín worsened. Wrath at having laid bare his heart before Helena and despair at the manner in which she had rejected him finally withered his soul. He succeeded in mastering himself for a time and he sought consolation in his wife and daughter. But his home life grew more somber, and he more bitter.

At this time he had a maid in his house who was very devout, who managed to attend Mass every day, and who passed every moment which domestic service permitted her shut up in her room saying her prayers. She went about with her eyes lowered and fixed on the ground, and she responded to everything with the greatest meekness, in a somewhat sniveling voice. Joaquín could not bear her, and was constantly scolding her without any pretext whatever. She habitually replied: "The master is right."

"What do you mean, I'm right?" Joaquín burst out on one occasion. "I'm not right at all!"

"Very well, sir, please do not be angered. You're not right then."

"Is that all?"

"I don't understand, sir."

"What do you mean, you don't understand, you prude, you hypocrite! Why don't you defend yourself? Why don't you answer back? Why don't you rebel?"

"Rebel? I, sir? God and the Blessed Virgin keep me from any rebellion, sir."

"What more can you want," interposed Antonia, "if she admits her own shortcomings?"

"She doesn't admit them at all. She is steeped in arrogance!"

"In arrogance, I, sir?"

"You see? The hypocrite is proud of not admitting anything. She is simply using me, at my expense, to do exercises in humility and patience. She uses my fits of temper as a kind of hair shirt to bring out in her the virtue of patience. At my expense, mind you! No, it shall not be; not at my expense. She can't use me as an instrument to pile up good marks in heaven! That's real hypocrisy for you!"

The poor little maid wept, as she prayed between her teeth.

"But, it's really true that she is humble. . . . Why should she rebel? If she *had* rebelled, you would have been even more irritated."

"No! It's a gross breach of faith to use the foibles of someone else as a means of exercising one's own virtue. Let her reply to me, let her be insolent, let her be a human being . . . and not just a servant. . . ."

"In which case, Joaquín, you would be much more annoyed."

"No, what really irritates me most are all these pretensions to greater perfection."

"You are mistaken, sir," said the maid without lifting her eyes from the ground; "I don't think I am better than anyone."

"You don't, eh? Well I do! And whoever doesn't think himself better than another is a fool. You probably think yourself the greatest woman sinner of all time, isn't that it? Come on now, answer me!"

"These things cannot be asked, sir."

"Come now, answer me, for they say that St. Louis Gonzaga believed himself the greatest sinner among men, and you, answer me yes or no, don't you think you're the greatest sinner among women?"

"The sins of other women are not on my soul, sir."

"Idiot! Worse than idiot! Get out of here!"

"God forgive you, as I do, sir!"

"For what? Come back and tell me. For what? What will God have to forgive me for? Come on, tell me!"

"Very well. For your sake, ma'am, I am sorry to go, but I shall leave this house."

"That's the way you should have begun. . . ." Joaquín concluded.

Later, alone with his wife, he said to her:

"Won't this innocent hypocrite go around now

saying that I am mad? Antonia, am I not, perhaps, mad? Tell me, am I mad, or not?"

"For God's sake, Joaquín, don't become. . . ."

"Yes, yes, I believe I am mad. . . . Send me away. All this will put an end to me."

"You must put an end to *it*."

CHAPTER 19

Joaquín now lavished all his ardor upon his daughter, in raising her, in educating her, in keeping her free of the world's immoralities.

"It's just as well she is the only one," he would say to his wife. "It's just as well that we didn't have another."

"Wouldn't you have liked a son?"

"No, no, a daughter is better; it's easier to isolate a girl from this vile world. Besides, if there had been two, jealousies would have developed between them. . . ."

"Oh, no!"

"Oh, yes! Affection cannot be divided equally between several: what is given one is taken away from another. Each one demands everything for himself, and for himself alone. No, no, I shouldn't want to see myself in God's plight. . . ."

"What is that, now?"

"The one of having so many children. Isn't it said that we are all children of God?"

"Don't say these things, Joaquín. . . ."

"There are well people so that there may be infirm. . . . One has only to look at the way illness is distributed!"

Joaquín did not want his daughter to have anything to do with people. He brought a private teacher to the house, and he himself, in moments of leisure, gave her instruction.

Joaquina, the poor girl, saw in her father an invalid, a sick man, a patient rather than a doctor. Meanwhile, from him she received a somber view of the world and of life.

"I tell you," Joaquín continued the argument with his wife, "that she is enough, alone, so that we need not divide our affections. . . ."

"They say that the more it is divided, the more it grows. . . ."

"Don't believe it. You remember poor Ramirez, the solicitor? His father had two sons and two daughters and very few resources. In their house they ate aperitifs and soup, but never an entree. Only the father, Ramirez senior, ate a main course; from time to time, he would share a little with one of the sons and one of the daughters, but never with the others. When they 'celebrated,' on special occasions, they were served two entrees to be divided among the family, plus one for him, since, as master of the house, he had to be distinguished in some way. The hierarchy had to be preserved. And at night, as he retired to sleep, Ramirez senior would kiss one of his sons and one of his daughters, but not the remaining two."

"How awful! Why did he do that?"

"How do I know? . . . Perhaps the two favorites looked more attractive. . . ."

"It sounds like the case of Carvajal who can't bear his youngest daughter. . . ."

"That's because the last child was born six years after the other and at a time when he was low in funds. She was just one more burden, an unexpected one. That's why they call her The Intruder."

"Good God, how horrible!"

"Such is life, Antonia, a seed-bed of horrors. And let us thank God that we don't have to distribute our affection."

"Don't say that!"

"I'll say no more."

And he made her be quiet too.

CHAPTER 20

Abel's son was studying medicine and his father made a habit of keeping Joaquín informed on the progress of the boy's studies. Joaquín himself spoke to the boy a few times and gradually grew attached to him, or simply "fond" of him, as he thought at the time.

"How does it happen that you prepare him for medicine instead of for painting?" Joaquín asked the father.

"I am not preparing him, he is preparing himself. He doesn't feel any vocation toward art. . . ."

"I see, and to study medicine one needs, of course, no 'vocation.' . . ."

"I didn't say that. You always take everything the worst way. He not only does not feel any vocation toward art, but he is not even curious about it. He scarcely stops to see what I am painting; nor does he inform himself about it."

"Perhaps it's better that way. . . ."

"Why do you say that?"

"Because if he had devoted himself to painting he would necessarily become a better or a worse painter than you. If worse, it would not do, nor could he have endured it, to be called, not merely Abel Sanchez, the younger, but Abel

Sanchez the Bad, or Sanchez the Bad, or Abel the Bad. . . ."

"And if he were better than I?"

"Then it would be you who could not endure it."

" 'The thief thinks that everyone else is a thief.' "

"Oh, that's it. Turn on me with an insult. No artist can tolerate the fame of another, especially if it is a son or brother. Better the fame of a stranger. That one of the same blood should triumph . . . never! How explain it? . . . You do well to train him for medicine."

"In any case, he will earn more."

"Do you mean to imply that you don't make a good income from painting?"

"I make something."

"Yes, and have fame besides."

"Fame? For whatever that's worth . . . as long as it lasts."

"Money doesn't last either."

"It's a little more substantial."

"Don't be a fraud, Abel, and pretend to despise fame."

"I assure you that what concerns me now is to leave my son a fortune."

"You will leave him a name."

"There is no market quotation on a name."

"On yours, there is!"

"On my signature, but it's only . . . Sanchez!

And he might very well decide to sign himself Abel S. Puig, or some such thing. Let him be Marquis of the house of Sanchez. The Abel takes away the sting from the Sanchez. And Abel Sanchez sounds well enough."

CHAPTER 21

In flight from himself, and, so as to suppress in his sick and melancholy consciousness that ever-present image of Abel which haunted him, Joaquín began to frequent a nightly gathering at his club. The light conversation would serve as a narcotic, and he hoped he might even be intoxicated by it. Do not some men give themselves up to drink so to drown the passion which devastates them, and to allow their frustrated love to flow away with the wine? And so he would give himself up to the talk in the club, listening rather more than taking an active part, so as to drown his passion.

Only, the remedy turned out to be worse than the ill.

He always went prepared to keep himself in restraint, to laugh and joke, to gossip pleasantly, to appear as a kind of disinterested spectator of life, generous as only a professed skeptic can be, heedful of the fact that to understand is to forgive, prepared never to allow the cancer of hatred which consumed his will to show through. But the evil escaped through his lips, in his words, when he least expected it, and the odor of wickedness was perceived by all. He would return home exasperated with himself, reproaching himself for cowardice and his lack of self-control, and would resolve to return no more to the club gatherings. "I will not go again," he would tell himself, "I must not. All this only worsens the matter, aggravates it. The ambient there is poisonous, the air is filled with suppressed evils and passions. No, I shall not return there. What I need is solitude, solitude. Blessed solitude!"

And yet he would go back.

He would go back because he was unable to endure his solitude. For in solitude he never managed to be alone, the other one was always present The other one! He went so far as to catch himself in a dialogue with him, supplying the other's words for him. The other, in these solitary dialogues, these monologues in dialogues, spoke to him without rancor of any kind, of indifferent matters, even sometimes of pleasant things. "My God, why doesn't he hate me?" Joaquín came to ask himself. "Why doesn't he hate me?"

One day he even found himself on the point of addressing God, of asking Him in a diabolic speech to infiltrate some hatred into Abel's heart, hatred toward himself, Joaquín. Another time he burst out: "Oh, if he only envied me . . . if he only envied me." And this idea, which flashed lividly across the black clouds of his bitter spirit, brought him a relaxing joy, a joy which caused him to tremble in the marrow of his shivering soul. "To be envied! . . . Only to be envied! . . ."

"But," he asked himself, "doesn't all this simply prove that I hate myself, that I envy myself?" He went to the door, locked it with a key, looked about him and, certain that he was alone, fell to his knees. In a voice scalded by tears he murmured: "Lord, you have told me to love my neighbor as myself, and I cannot love him at all, for I don't love myself, I don't know how to love myself, I cannot love myself. What have you done with me, Lord?"

He went then and got his Bible, and opened it to where it reads: "And Jehovah said to Cain: Where is thy brother Abel?" Slowly he closed the book, murmuring: "And where am I?"

At this moment he heard sounds outside, and he hastened to open the door. "Papa! Papa!" his daughter was joyfully shouting, as she came in. Her fresh, young voice seemed to bring him back into the light. He kissed the girl and then, grazing her ear with his lips he told her in a low voice, so that no one else might hear: "Pray for your father, my daughter."

"Father, Father!" cried the girl, throwing her arms about his neck.

He hid his head in the girl's shoulder and burst into tears.

"What is the matter, Papa, are you sick?"

"Yes, I am sick. . . . But you mustn't ask any more."

CHAPTER 22

And he returned to the club. It was useless to fight against going back. Every day he invented another pretext for going. And the mill of conversation continued to grind.

One of the figures there was Federico Cuadrado, an implacable man, who, when he heard anyone speak well of another would ask: "Against whom is that eulogy directed?"

"I can't be fooled," he would say in his small, cold, cutting voice. "When someone is vigorously praised, the speaker always has someone else in mind whom he is trying to debase with this eulogy, a second someone who is a rival to the praised party. This is true when it's not a matter of deliberately trying to vent one's scorn on the person mentioned. . . . You can be sure that no one eulogizes with good intentions."

"Wait a minute," interjected León Gómez, who took a great delight in making the cynic talk; "there's Don Leovigildo, now, whom no one has ever heard say a word against another. . . ."

"Well," a provincial deputy put in, "the fact is Don Leovigildo is a politician, and politicians must remain on good terms with everybody. What do you say, Federico?"

"I say that Don Leovigildo will die without having spoken badly or thought well of any man. . . . He would not give, perhaps, the slightest little push to send another sprawling, even if no one were to see it, because he not only fears the penal code, but also hell. But if the other person falls and breaks his crown, he will feel delight to his very marrow. And, in order to enjoy his pleasure in the broken skull, he will be the first to go and offer his sympathy and condolences."

"I don't know how it is possible to live with such sentiments," interposed Joaquín.

"What sentiments?" Federico caught him up. "Don Leovigildo's, mine, or yours?"

"No one has mentioned me in this conversation!"; Joaquin spoke with acid displeasure.

"I do, now, my good fellow, for we all know each other here. . . ."

Joaquín felt himself turn pale. The phrase "My good fellow," which Federico, inspired by his guardian devil, lightly bestowed upon anyone into whom he got his hooks, had pierced Joaquín in his innermost will.

"I can't understand why you have such an aversion for Don Leovigildo," blurted Joaquín, who was sorry as soon as he had spoken, for he felt he was poking a sputtering, dangerous fire.

"Aversion? Aversion, I? For Don Leovigildo?"

"Yes. . . . I don't know what harm he could have done you."

"In the first place, my good fellow, it is not necessary for someone to harm you for you to take a dislike to him. When you have a dislike for someone, an 'aversion,' it becomes easy to invent some harmful or malevolent action, that is to say, to imagine that the harm has been done one. . . . In the second place, I don't have any greater 'aversion' for Don Leovigildo than I have for anyone else whomsoever. He's a man, and that's enough. Moreover, he's an 'honorable' man!"

"Just as you are a professional misanthrope. . . ." began the provincial deputy.

"Man is the rottenest and most indecent vermin there is; I've said so a thousand times. And the 'honorable' man is the worst of the lot."

"Come on now," said León Gómez; and then, addressing the deputy: "What do you say to that, you who were talking the other day about honorable politicians, referring to Don Leovigildo?"

"An honorable politician," Federico burst out. "Oh, no, not that! That's completely impossible!"

"Why," exclaimed three voices at once.

"Why, you ask? Because he himself has belied it in his own words. He had the audacity in the course of a speech he was delivering to call himself honorable. And it is not honorable to declare oneself so. The Gospel says that Christ our Lord . . ."

"Don't mention Christ, I beg you!" Joaquín interrupted him.

"What, does Christ hurt you too, my good fellow?"

There was a short silence, sombre and cold.

"Christ our Lord," reiterated Federico, "said that he should not be called good, for only God is good. And yet there are Christian swine who dare to call themselves honorable."

"*Honorable* is not exactly the same as *good,*" interpolated Don Vicente, the magistrate.

"Ah, now you have said it yourself, Don Vicente. Thank the Lord for the opportunity to hear a sentence like that, both reasonable and just, from a magistrate!"

"So that one must not confess oneself to be honorable, is that it?" asked Joaquín. "But how about confessing oneself a rogue?"

"That isn't necessary."

"What Señor Cuadrado wants," said Don Vicente, the magistrate, "is for men to confess themselves scoundrels, and continue on in their normal course, isn't that it?"

"Bravo!" exclaimed the provincial deputy.

"I shall tell you, my good fellow," answered Federico, considering his reply. "You must certainly know what constitutes the excellence of the sacrament of confession in our most wise mother the Church. . . ."

"Some other barbarity, now," interrupted the magistrate.

"Barbarity not at all, but a very wise institution. Confession allows more graceful, more tranquil sinning, since one knows that one's sins will be forgiven. Isn't that so, Joaquín?"

"Yet, if one does not repent . . ."

"Oh, yes, my good fellow, yes, one must repent, and then again sin and once again repent, knowing while one is sinning that one will repent, and knowing when one repents that one will sin again, so that finally one is both sinning and repenting at the same time. Isn't that true?"

"Man is a mystery," said León Gómez.

"There is no need for inanities!" replied Federico.

"Why is that inane?"

"Any 'philosophical' maxim, stated just like that, any off-hand maxim, any solemn, general statement, put in the form of an aphorism, results in an inanity."

"And philosophy, then?"

"There is no other philosophy than what we are doing here right now. . . ."

"You mean flaying our fellow men?"

"Exactly. Man is best when flayed."

After the club gathering, Federico approached Joaquín to ask if he were going home, for he would have liked to accompany him for a short distance; but when Joaquín told him he was not going home, but simply going on a visit close by, Federico said:

"I understand. The business about the visit is simply a blind. What you want is to be left alone. I understand."

"How do you understand it?"

"One is never better off than when one is alone. But, when solitude weighs on you, call upon me. You will find no one who will better distract you from your burdens."

"What about your own?" Joaquín blurted out.

"Bah! Who cares about them?" . . .

Whereupon they parted company.

CHAPTER 23

There roamed about the city a poor needy man, an Aragonese, father of five children, who earned a living as best he could, as a scribe or at whatever turned up. The poor man frequently appealed to friends—if such men as he can indeed be said to have any—petitioning them under a thousand pretexts for the advance of two or three five-peseta notes. The saddest aspect of the whole thing was that he sometimes sent around one of his children, or even his wife, who appeared at the homes of acquaintances bearing little begging letters. Joaquín had occasionally helped him, especially when he had sent for him as a doctor to treat someone in his family. For Joaquín found a singular satisfaction in helping the poor man; he saw in him a victim of human badness.

One time Joaquín asked Abel about him.

"Yes, I know him," the latter said. "I even gave him work for a while. But he's an idler, a vagrant. With the excuse that he is drowning his sorrows, he doesn't let a day go by without showing up at the cafe, even though at home the stove can't be lit. Nor will he be without his little package of cigarettes. He wants to turn his troubles into smoke."

"That isn't the whole story, Abel. It would be necessary to examine the case from within. . . ."

"Listen, don't be absurd. Something I can't tolerate is that line about 'I'll return this loan as soon as I can. . . .' Let him ask for alms and be done with it! It would be more open and noble. The last time, he asked me for fifteen pesetas and I gave him five, but told him: 'Not to be paid back!' He's a loafer!"

"How can you blame him? . . ."

"Come now, here we go again: 'Whose fault is it?' "

"Exactly! Whose fault *is* it?"

"All right, then. Let's forget it. If you want to help him, please do so; I won't stand in the way. I'm sure that I myself will, if he asks me again, give him what he wants."

"I knew that without your telling me, for underneath it all you are. . . ."

"Let's not go 'underneath it all.' I am a painter and I don't paint the person underneath. Even more, I'm convinced that all men wear outside everything that they are inside."

"Well, then, for you, a man is no more than a painter's model. . . ."

"Does that seem a small matter to you? For you, he is no more than a sick man, a patient. You're the one who goes about looking into men, auscultating them, listening in. . . ."

"Yes, it's a piddling business. . . ."

"How so?"

"And then, when one is habituated to looking into people, one ends by looking into oneself, auscultating oneself, listening in. . . ."

"There's an advantage in that. I've had enough when I look at myself in the mirror. . . ."

"Have you ever really looked at yourself in the mirror?"

"Naturally! You must know that I've painted a self portrait."

"A masterpiece, no doubt. . . ."

"Well now, it's not altogether bad. . . . And you, have you examined yourself thoroughly?"

The day following this conversation Joaquín left the club with Federico because he wanted to ask the latter if he knew the poor man who roamed about begging in a shameful fashion. "And tell me the truth, now, for we're alone. None of your ferocious statements."

"Well look; he's a poor devil who should be in jail, where he would at least eat better than he does and where he would live more calmly."

"But what has he done?"

"No; he hasn't done anything; he should have; and that's why I say he should be in jail."

"What is it he should have done?"

"Killed his brother."

"Now you're starting up again!"

"I shall explain it to you. This poor man is, as you know, from the province of Aragon, and there, in his native region, absolute liberty in disposing of property still exists. He had the misfortune to be the first born son and legitimate heir, and then he had the misfortune to fall in love with a poor girl, comely and honorable though she was to all appearances. The father opposed their relationship with all his might, threatening to disinherit him if he went so far as to marry the girl. And our man, blind with love, first compromised the girl seriously, thinking thus to convince the father, and ended by marrying her and leaving home. He stayed on in the town, working as best he might at the home of his in-laws, hoping to soften his father. And the latter, a good Aragonese, grew more and more unyielding; and died disinheriting the poor devil and leaving his estate to the second son; and a rather fair-sized estate it was, too. When his in-laws died a little while later, the poor man appealed to his brother for help and work; and his brother denied him; and, so as not to kill this false brother—which is what his natural anger urged him to do—he has come here to live from alms and caging. This, then, is the story; as you see, very edifying."

"So very edifying!"

"Had he killed his brother, that species of Jacob, it would have been an evil; and not killing him, an evil too. . . . Perhaps a worse one."

"Don't say that, Federico."

"It's true, for he not only lives wretchedly and shamefully, a parasite, but he lives hating his brother."

"And if he had killed him?"

"Then he would have been cured of his hatred, and today, repentant of his crime, he would be honoring his brother's memory. Action liberates one and dissipates poisoned sentiment, and it is poisoned sentiment which sickens the soul. Believe me, Joaquín, for I know it very well."

Joaquín looked at him deliberately:

"And you?" he thrust out.

"I? You wouldn't want to know things that don't concern you, would you, my boy? Let it be enough for you to know that all my cynicism is defensive. I am not the son of the man everyone takes to be my father; I am the child of an adultery, and there is no one in this world whom I hate worse than my own father, my illegitimate father, who was the executioner of the other one, the father who out of cowardice and baseness gave me his name, this indecent name which I bear."

"Still, the father is not the one who begets, but the one who raises the offspring. . . ."

"The truth is that this other father, the one you think has raised me, did no such thing, but instead weaned me on the venom of hatred which he bears my natural father, who engendered me and forced him to marry my mother."

CHAPTER 24

The course of study pursued by Abelin, Abel's son, came to an end, and the father called on Joaquín to see if he would take on his son to practice with him as his assistant. Joaquín accepted the boy.

I accepted him,—Joaquín wrote later in the *Confession* dedicated to his daughter—*from a strange mixture of curiosity, abhorrence of his father, and affection for the boy (who at that time seemed to me to be a mediocrity) coupled with a desire to free myself by this means from my evil passion. At the same time, deeper down in my heart, my demon whispered that the failure of the son would negate the pre-eminence of the father. So that on the one hand, I wanted to redeem myself of my hatred for the father by my affection for the son, and, on the other, I took a secret delight in anticipating that though Abel Sanchez triumphed in painting, another Abel Sanchez of his own blood would fail in medicine. I never would have been able at that time to imagine how deep a love I would come to feel for the son of the man who embittered and darkened the life of my spirit.*

And thus it came to pass that Joaquín and the son of Abel felt drawn to each other. Abelin was quick-witted and he avidly followed the precepts of Joaquín, whom he addressed as "maestro." His teacher proposed to make a good doctor of him, entrusting him with the wealth of his clinical experience. "I will lead him," he told himself, "to make the discoveries which this misbegotten restlessness of spirit has prevented me from making."

"Maestro," Abelin addressed him one day, "why don't you assemble all the scattered observations, all the random notes you have shown me, and write a book? It would be enormously interesting and highly instructive. There are scatterings of genius throughout the material, and extraordinary scientific wisdom."

"The truth is, son (it was thus he habitually addressed him), that I can't, I simply cannot. . . . I don't have the taste for it, I don't have the will, the courage, the serenity, the I-don't-know-what . . ."

"It would merely be a question of getting started. . . ."

"Yes, son, of course; it would merely be a question of getting started, but as many times as I've thought of it I've never come to the point of decision. To set myself to write a book . . . here in Spain . . . on medicine . . . ! No, it's not worth the effort. It would fall in the void. . . ."

"No, your work would not, I am sure of it."

"What I should have done is precisely what you must do: abandon this insufferable clientele and dedicate yourself to pure research, to true science, to physiology, histology, pathology, and not to the paying sick. You, who have some little means—your father's paintings must assure you of some—devote yourself to that."

"You may well be right, sir; but this does not alter the fact that you ought to publish your memoirs as a diagnostician."

"Look! If you want, we will arrange something. I will give you my notes, all of them. I will amplify them orally, I will answer all your questions. And you will publish the book. Does that appeal to you?"

"Wonderful! It would be wonderful. I have taken notes, ever since I have been assisting here, of everything I have heard and learned."

"Very well, my son, very well." And he embraced the boy with deep feeling.

Later, Joaquín said to himself: "This boy shall be my handiwork! Mine, and not his father's. In the end he will venerate me and understand that I am more worthy than his father, that there is more art in my practice of medicine than in his father's painting. And then, I will take him away from Abel, yes, I will take him away from him. He took Helena away from me, and I will take away his son from him. Abelin will become my son, and who knows? . . . perhaps he will finally renounce his father, when he finally knows him and finds out what he did to me."

CHAPTER 25

"But tell me," Joaquín asked his disciple one day, "how did you really come to study medicine?"

"I am not sure. . . ."

"Because it would have been most natural for you to have been attracted to painting. Young men usually feel called upon to practice their fathers' professions; from a spirit of emulation . . . the very ambient . . ."

"Painting never did interest me."

"Your father told me . . ."

"My father's painting even less."

"What do you mean by that?"

"I don't feel it, and I don't know whether he does either. . . ."

"That's a large statement. Would you explain? . . ."

"There is no one to hear what I say, and you, sir, you are like a second father to me . . . a second . . . Well, then. . . . Besides, you are his oldest friend, before you had either one reached the age of reason, and you are almost like brothers. . . ."

"Yes, yes, that's true enough. Abel and I are like brothers. . . . Go on."

"Well, then, today I would like to open my heart to you."

"Do so. Whatever you tell me will never be known."

"Yes, the truth is that I doubt that my father has any feeling for what he paints—or for anything else. He paints like a machine. He has a natural gift for it. But feeling? . . ."

"This is what I have always believed."

"Why, it was you, according to everyone, who contributed the largest impetus to his fame with that famous address which is still spoken of."

"How else could I have spoken?"

"That is what I say to myself. In any case, I think that my father feels neither painting nor anything else. He is made of cork."

"I wouldn't say that, son."

"Yes, cork. He lives only for his own glory. All that talk about his despising fame is a farce, pure farce. On the contrary, he seeks only applause. And he is an egotist, a perfect egotist. He doesn't love anyone else."

"Well, now . . . no one else . . . that's pretty strong."

"It's true, no one else. I don't even know how he came to marry my mother. I doubt that it was for love."

Joaquín turned pale.

"I know," the youth continued, "that he has had entanglements and affairs with some of his models. But they have been a matter of caprice and a little bit of showing off. He doesn't really care for anyone."

"But it seems to me that you are the one who should. . . ."

"He has never paid any attention to me. He has supported me, has paid for my education and studies, he has not stinted nor does he now stint me with respect to money. And still, I scarcely exist as far as he is concerned. Whenever I have asked him something, in regard to history, art, technique, painting, his travels, or anything else, he has said to me: 'Leave me alone, leave me in peace.' Once he said: 'Learn it yourself! Learn it, as I did! There are the books.' How different that is from you!"

"It might be that he didn't know, my son. Parents sometimes act unjustly towards their children simply because they do not want to admit they are more ignorant or slow than the youngsters."

"No, it wasn't that. . . . And there is something worse."

"Worse? What could it be?"

"Yes, worse. He has never reprimanded me, no matter what I may have done. Although I am not, nor ever have been, either dissolute or wild, still everyone who is young has his slips and falls. Nevertheless, he has never inquired into them and, even if he knew about them, has said nothing."

"That shows respect for your integrity, confidence in you. . . . It is probably the most generous and noble way to bring up a son, and demonstrates faith. . . ."

"No, it is nothing like that, in this case. It is simply indifference."

"Don't exaggerate, it isn't indifference. . . .

What could he say to you that your conscience wouldn't already have told you? A father can't be a judge."

"But he can be comrade, an adviser, a friend or teacher like you."

"And yet there are things which decorum forbids mentioning between father and son."

"It is only natural that you, his greatest and oldest friend, almost his brother, should defend him even though . . ."

"Even though what?"

"May I tell you everything?"

"Yes, tell everything."

"Well then, I have never heard him speak otherwise than well of you, too well, but . . ."

"But what?"

"That's just it. He speaks too well of you."

"What do you mean by speaking too well?"

"For instance, before I came to know you, I thought of you as someone completely different than you are."

"Explain yourself."

"For my father you are a kind of tragic being, with a soul tortured by profound passions. 'If one might only paint the soul of Joaquín,' he has often said. He speaks as if there were a secret operating between you and him. . . ."

"These are merely suspicions of yours. . . ."

"No, they are not."

"And your mother?"

"Ah, my mother . . ."

CHAPTER 26

"Listen, Joaquín," Antonia said to her husband one day, "it seems to me that one of these fine days our daughter will leave us, or be taken away from us. . . ."

"Joaquina? Where to?"

"To the convent!"

"Impossible!"

"On the contrary, highly possible. You have simply been engrossed in your own affairs, and now you are taken up with this son of Abel's, whom you seem to have adopted. . . . Anyone would say you were more fond of him than of your own daughter. . . ."

"The point is that I am trying to save him, to redeem him from his antecedents. . . ."

"No, what you are really trying to do is to take revenge. How vengeful you are! You neither forgive nor forget! I fear that God will punish you, will punish us. . . ."

"Oh, and is that the reason Joaquina wants to enter a convent?"

"I didn't say that."

"But I do, and that's the same thing. Is she going because she is jealous of Abelin? Is she afraid that I will grow to love him more than I do her? Because if that's the reason . . ."

"That is not the reason."

"What, then?"

"I don't know. . . . She says she has a vocation, that God calls her there. . . ."

"God? God? Her confessor, more likely. Who is he?"

"Father Echevarria."

"The one who was my confessor?"

"The same."

Joaquín seemed crestfallen. He began to muse. On the following day he called his wife aside and told her:

"I believe I have uncovered the motives for Joaquina's impulse to enter the cloister, or rather, the motives for Father Echevarria's inducing her to become a nun. Do you remember how I sought help and refuge in the church against that wretched obsession which takes possession of my whole soul, against that spitefulness which through the years grows older—harder and more stubborn, and do you remember how, despite all my efforts, I did not succeed in my purpose. No, Father Echevarria did not give me any help, he could not. For that evil there is no remedy but one, only one."

He was silent for a moment, as if expecting a question from his wife, and, as she kept quiet, he went on:

"For that evil there is no remedy but death. Who knows? . . . I was almost born with him, and perhaps I shall die with him. Well then, this little priestling, who could not help me nor convert me, is now, without a doubt, pushing my daughter, your daughter, our daughter, toward the convent, so that there she may pray for me, so that she may save me by sacrificing herself. . . ."

"But it is not a sacrifice . . . she says it is her vocation. . . ."

"That's not true, Antonia; it's a lie. Most of those who become nuns, do so to escape work, to lead a poor, but easy life, a mystic *siesta.* Either that, or they are running away from home. Our daughter is running away from home, from us."

"It must be from you. . . ."

"Yes, she is running away from me. She has guessed my secret!"

"And now that you have formed this attachment for that . . ."

"Do you mean to tell me that she is running away from him too?"

"From your capriciousness, your new caprice. . . ."

"Caprice? Caprice, you say? I am anything but capricious, Antonia. I take everything seriously, everything, do you understand?"

"Yes, too seriously," added the woman, dissolving into tears.

"Come now, don't cry, Antonia, my little saint.

my good angel, and forgive me if I have said anything. . . ."

"What you say isn't the worst, it's what you don't say."

"Listen, for God's sake, Antonia, for God's sake, see to it that our daughter doesn't leave us. If she goes into a convent, it will kill me; yes, it will kill me, it will simply kill me. Make her stay here, and I will do whatever she wants . . . if she wants me to send Abelin away, to dismiss him, I will do it. . . ."

"I remember when you said you were glad we had only the one daughter, because that way we did not have to divide our affections or spread them. . . ."

"But I don't divide them!"

"Something worse then. . . ."

"Antonia, our daughter wants to sacrifice herself for my sake, and she doesn't know that if she enters a convent she will leave me in despair. This house is her convent!"

CHAPTER 27

Two days later Joaquín took counsel in his study with his wife and daughter.

"Papa, it's God's desire!" Joaquina said to him resolutely, gazing at him squarely.

"It isn't God who wants it, but that little priestling of yours," her father replied. "How does a kid like you know what God wants? When have you communicated with Him?"

"I go to Communion every week, Father."

"And you think the attacks of dizziness which come from your fasting stomach are revelations from God?"

"A fasting heart breeds worse delusions."

"This decision cannot stand. God doesn't want it, He can't. I tell you He can't want it!"

"I don't know what God wants, but you, Father, know what He doesn't want, is that it? You may know a good deal about things of the body, but about things of God, of the soul . . ."

"Of the soul, is it? So you think I know nothing of the soul?"

"Perhaps you know something it would be better not to know."

"Are you accusing me?"

"No. It is you, Father, who accuse yourself."

"You see, Antonia, do you see, didn't I tell you?"

"And what did he tell you, Mama?"

"Nothing, my child, nothing. Suspicions and imaginings of your father. . . ."

"Well, then," exclaimed Joaquín, like a man who has come to a decision, "you are entering a convent in order to save me, isn't that true?"

"Perhaps you are not too far from the truth."

"And what is it you want to save me from?"

"I am not sure."

"Would I know? . . . From what, from whom?"

"From whom, Father, from whom? Why, from the devil or from yourself."

"And what do you know about it?"

"For God's sake, Joaquín, for God's sake. . . ." Antonia's voice was tearful; she was frightened by her husband's tone and appearance.

"Leave us, leave us alone, she and I. This does not concern you!"

"How can it not concern me? . . . She is my daughter. . . ."

"She's mine, you mean! She's a Monegro, and I'm a Monegro. Leave us. You don't understand, you couldn't understand these things. . . ."

"Father, if you continue to treat Mother in this way in front of me, I am leaving. Don't cry, Mother."

"But do you believe, my daughter . . . ?"

"What I believe, and know, is that I am as much his daughter as yours."

"As much?"

"Perhaps more."

"Don't talk like that, for God's sake," the mother burst out, in tears, "if you go on I will leave the room."

"That would be best," added the daughter. "Alone, we would better be able to see each other's face, or rather souls, we Monegros."

The mother stopped to kiss her daughter before leaving the room.

"Well now," began the father coldly, as soon as he found himself alone with his daughter, "to save me from what or whom are you going to a convent?"

"From whom or from what I don't know, Father; I know only that you must be saved. I don't know either what is wrong in this house, between you and my mother, I don't know what is wrong with you, but there is certainly something wrong. . . ."

"Did the little priestling tell you that?"

"No, the little priestling did not tell me that; he hasn't had to tell me; no one has told me, I have simply breathed it in since I was born. Here in this house we live as if in spiritual darkness!"

"Nonsense! That's something you've read in a book!"

"Just as you have read other things in your books. Or do you really believe that only those books which deal with the insides of the body, those books of yours with the ugly illustrations, are the ones to teach the truth?"

"Very well. And this spiritual darkness which you talk about, what is it?"

"You should know better than I, Father. In any case, don't deny that something is taking place here, that a sadness hangs over us like a black cloud and penetrates everywhere, that you are never satisfied and are suffering, as if you bore a great weight on your back. . . ."

"Yes; original sin," said Joaquín maliciously.

"Truer than you think," answered his daughter. "You haven't yet expiated it."

"I was baptized. . . ."

"That doesn't make any difference."

"And as a remedy for all this you propose to stick yourself in a nunnery, is that it? Well, the first thing to have done would have been to find out what the cause was. . . ."

"God forbid that I should judge you and my mother."

"But you don't object to condemning me?"

"Condemn you?"

"Yes, condemn me; your going off in this fashion is a condemnation. . . ."

"What if I went off with a husband? If I left you for a man? . . ."

"It depends on the man."

There was a brief silence.

"The truth is, my daughter, I am not well," Joaquín resumed. "I do suffer, I have been suffering nearly all my life. There is a good deal of truth in what you have guessed. Nevertheless, your decision to become a nun is the finishing blow, it exacerbates and heightens my pain. Have compassion on your father, your bedeviled father. . . ."

"It's from compassion. . . ."

"No, it's from egotism. You're running away. You see me suffer and you run away. It's egotism, indifference, lack of affection which leads you to the cloister. Suppose that I had a contagious and long-lasting disease, leprosy for example, would you leave me to go off to the convent and pray God to cure me? . . . Come now, answer, would you leave me?"

"No, I wouldn't leave you; I'm your only child, after all."

"Well, imagine that I am a leper. Stay and cure me. I'll place myself in your care, and do what you order."

"If that's the way it is. . . ."

The father rose and gazed an instant at his daughter through his tears before he embraced her. Then, holding her in his arms he whispered in her ear:

"Do you want to cure me, my daughter?"

"Yes, Papa."

"Then marry Abelin."

"What!" exclaimed the girl, detaching herself from her father and staring into his face.

"Does it surprise you?" stammered the father, surprised in his turn.

"Me, marry Abelin, the son of your enemy? . . ."

"Who called him that?"

"Your silence through past years."

"Well, that's the reason—because he is the son of the man you call my enemy."

"I don't know what there is between you, I don't want to know, but lately . . . seeing how you grew attached to his son, I became frightened, I feared . . . I don't know what. To me your affection for Abelin seemed monstrous, something infernal. . . ."

"No, my daughter, it was not that. In him I sought redemption. And believe me, if you succeed in bringing him into my house, if you make him my son, it will be as if the sun were at last to shine in my soul. . . ."

"But do you, my father, want me to court him, to solicit him?"

"I don't say that."

"Well, then? . . ."

"If he . . ."

"Ah, so you already had it planned between the two of you, without consulting me?"

"No, I hadn't thought it out, I, your father, your poor father, I . . ."

"You grieve me, Father."

"I grieve myself. And now I am responsible for everything. Weren't you thinking of sacrificing yourself for me?"

"That's true, yes, I will sacrifice myself for you. Ask whatever you like of me!"

The father went to kiss her, but she, breaking away from him, exclaimed:

"No, not now! When you deserve it. Or do you want me, too, to quiet you with kisses?"

"Where did you hear that, Daughter?"

"Walls have ears."

"And accusing tongues!"

CHAPTER 28

"Ah, to be you, Don Joaquín," said the poor disinherited Aragonese father of five to Joaquín one day, after he had succeeded in extracting some money from his benefactor.

"You want to be me! I don't understand."

"Yes, I would give everything to be you, Don Joaquín."

"What is this 'everything' you would give, now?"

"Everything I can give, everything I have."

"And what is that?"

"My life!"

"Your life to be me!" To himself Joaquín added: "I would give my own to be someone else entirely!"

"Yes, my life in order to be you."

"This is something I can't very well understand, my friend. I can't understand anyone's being disposed to give up their life to be someone else. To be someone else is to cease to be oneself, to cease to be the person one is."

"Doubtless so."

"Which is the same as ceasing to exist."

"Doubtless."

"And with no guarantee of becoming another . . ."

"Doubtless. What I mean to say, Don Joaquín, is that I would cease to exist, with a very good will, or more clearly, that I would put a bullet in my head or throw myself in the river, if I could be sure that my family, who keep me tied to this miserable life, who don't allow me to take my life, would find a father in you. Don't you understand now?"

"Yes I do understand. So that . . ."

". . . a wretched bit of attachment I have to this life! I would be very glad to give up being myself and to kill off my memories, if it were not for my family. Although, in truth, there is something else which restrains me, too."

"What?"

"The fear that my memories, my story, my history might accompany me beyond death. Ah, to be you!"

"And suppose motives just like your own, my friend, keep me alive?"

"Impossible, you're rich."

"Rich . . . rich . . ."

"A rich man never has cause for complaint. You lack nothing. A wife, daughter, a good practice, reputation . . . what more could you want? You weren't disinherited by your father; you weren't put out of your house to beg by your brother. You weren't obliged to become a beggar! Ah, to be you, Don Joaquín!"

When Don Joaquín found himself alone later he said to himself: "Ah, to be me! That man actually envies me, he envies *me!* And I, who would I like to be?"

CHAPTER 29

A few days later Abelin and Joaquina were betrothed. And, in the *Confession,* dedicated to his daughter, Joaquín not long afterwards wrote:

It is scarcely possible, my daughter, to explain to you how I brought Abel, your present husband, to the point of proposing to you. I had to make him think you were in love with him or at least wanted him to be in love with you; I had to do this without the slightest hint of the talk you and I had held when your mother told me you wanted to enter a convent for my sake. I saw my salvation in this marriage. Only by linking your fate with that of young Abel, the son of the man who had poisoned the fountain of my life, only by mixing our two blood lines could there be any hope for my salvation.

And yet, it occurred to me that perhaps your children, my grandchildren, the children of his children, his grandchildren, the heirs to our blood, might some day find themselves warring within themselves, bearing hatred in their seed. Still, I thought, isn't hatred toward oneself, toward one's very blood brother, the only remedy against hating others? The Scripture says that Esau and Jacob were already fighting in the womb of Rebecca. Who knows but that some day you will conceive twins, one with my blood and the other with his and that they will hate each other and fight, beginning in your womb, before coming out into the air and into consciousness. This is the human tragedy, and like Job, every man is a child of contradictions.

And I have trembled to think that I had perhaps joined you together, not for a union of your blood, but instead to separate the two lines even more and perpetuate a hatred. Forgive me! . . . I am prey to a certain delirium.

But it is not only my blood and his that are involved; there is also Helena's. . . . The blood of Helena! This is what most disturbs me: the blood which flowers in her cheeks, her forehead, her lips, that sets off her glance; that blinded me through the tissue of her skin!

And then there is another blood line . . . Antonia's; the blood of the unfortunate Antonia, your blessed mother. This blood is like baptismal water. It is the blood of redemption. Only your mother's blood, Joaquina, can save your children, our grandchildren. It is this spotless blood which can redeem us.

Antonia must never see this journal; she must not see it. Let her leave this world, if she outlives me, without having more than guessed at our mystery—and our corruptibility.

The betrothed quickly grew to understand and appreciate each other and to feel genuine affection. They came to realize that each was a victim of his own home, and of their individual ambients, both unfortunate: the one home frivolous and unfeeling, the other impassioned and stifling. They both sought support in Antonia. They felt a profound impulse to establish a home, a center of serene and self-sufficient love, of love which would be all-encompassing and would not romantically fix its gaze elsewhere or moon after other loves; their need was for a castle of solitude, where love could unite the two unfortunate families. They would make Abel, the painter, come to realize that the intimate life of the home is an imperishable reality of which art is but a bright reflection, when it is not a shadow. They would show Helena that perpetual youth is the property of the spirit able to submerge itself in the vital current of the family and its inheritance. Joaquín would be made to realize that although name and identity are lost with the loss of one's blood they are lost only to be joined in the new name and the new blood.

Antonia did not need to be shown anything, for she was a woman who had been born to live in the sweetness of custom.

Joaquín did in fact undergo a rebirth. He spoke of his old friend Abel with emotion and affection, and even confessed that it had been a stroke of good fortune to have lost Helena once and for all through Abel's intervention.

One time when he and his daughter were alone, he told her: "Now that everything seems to be taking a different and better turn, I can speak quite frankly. I did, at one time, love Helena. Or, at least I thought I did, and I courted her, to no avail. And the truth is she never gave me the slightest reason to hope for anything. Then I introduced her to Abel, who will now be your father-in-law, your second father, and the two of them were immediately drawn together. I took the entire episode as an affront, a mortal insult. . . . But what right did I have to her?"

"That's true. But men are like that in their demands."

"You're right, Daughter. I have acted like a madman, brooding upon a fancied insult, an imagined betrayal. . . ."

"Is that all, Father?"

"How do you mean, is that all?"

"Is that all there was to it, nothing more?"

"To my knowledge . . . no!" But as he said this, he closed his eyes and was unable to control the beating of his heart.

"Now you will be married," he went on, "and you will live with me. Yes, you will live with me, and I will make your husband—my new son—a great doctor, an artist in medicine, a complete artist, who at the very least will equal his father's fame."

"And he will record your work as he has told me."

"Yes, he will write what I have not been able to. . . ."

"He has told me that your career has demonstrated genius and that you have developed practices and made discoveries. . . ."

"Adulation on his part. . . ."

"He has told me privately. You are not known, not esteemed at your true worth, and he wants to write this account so that your work will become known."

"High time, at that. . . ."

"If fortune is good, it's never too late."

"Ah, Daughter, if instead of burying myself in patients, in this cursed practice which doesn't allow time to breathe or learn, if instead I had devoted myself to pure science, to research, the discovery for which Dr. Alvarez y García is so much lauded would have been my work, for I was on the verge of developing it. But this business of working for a living . . ."

"We weren't in straits, you didn't have to do it."

"Yes, but . . . I don't know. Anyway, it's all past now and a new life begins. Now I shall give up my practice."

"Really and truly?"

"Yes, I shall give it over to your future husband, and simply keep an eye on how it goes. I shall lend him a guiding hand, and I will devote myself to my own work. We will all live together, and make another life. I can begin to live again, and I will be another man, another person. . . ."

"What a pleasure it is to hear you talk this way, Father. At last!"

"Does it please you to hear that I shall be another person?"

Joaquín's daughter looked at him closely as she sensed the undertones implicit in the question.

"Does it make you happy to hear that I shall be someone else?" the father asked the girl again.

"Yes, Father, it makes me happy!"

"In other words, the actual person, the person that I really am, strikes you as unfortunate?"

"And how does it strike you, Father?" the girl asked him resolutely, in her turn.

"Oh, don't let me say any more," he cried out.

And his daughter stopped his mouth with a kiss.

CHAPTER 30

"You already know why I've come," Abel said to Joaquín as soon as they were alone in the latter's office.

"Yes, I know. Your son has announced your visit."

"My son and soon yours. You don't know how happy it makes me. This is the way our friendship should culminate. My son is now nearly yours too. He already loves you as he would a father, and not just as a teacher. I'm ready to assert that he loves you more than he does me. . . ."

"No, no, not that. Don't say that."

"And what of it? Do you think I am jealous? I am incapable of jealousy. And listen, Joaquín, if there has been something standing between us before . . ."

"Please, Abel, don't say any more about . . ."

"I must. Now that our two blood lines will be united, now that my son is to become yours, and your daughter is to become mine, we must settle that old score. We must be absolutely frank."

"No, no, nothing of the kind. And if you talk of it I'll leave."

"All right, then. But in any case I shall not forget what you said about my work the night of the supper."

"I wish you wouldn't talk about that either."

"About what shall I talk then?"

"Nothing of the past; nothing. Let's talk only about the future. . . ."

"Well, if you and I, at our age, are not to talk of the past, what are we to talk of? Why, we haven't anything left but the past."

"Don't say that," Joaquín almost cried out.

"We can't live now except from memories."

"Abel, please be quiet."

"And if the truth were known, it's better to live from memories than from hopes. The former have same basis in fact, but the latter . . . one cannot even know whether they'll ever be."

"But let's not go over our past," Joaquín insisted.

"We can talk of our children, then; in short, of our hopes."

"That's it. Let's talk of them, rather than of ourselves. . . ."

"In you my boy will have a teacher and a father. . . ."

"In any case, I hope to leave him my practice, give him at least those patients who are willing to make the change and whom I have already prepared for it. In acute cases I will be there to assist."

"Wonderful. Thank you, thank you."

"Then I will also give Joaquina a dowry. But they will live with me."

"My son has already told me. Still, I think it would be better if they had their own home: there is no house big enough for two families."

"No, I cannot be apart from my daughter."

"But you think we can live apart from our son, is that it?"

"You already live apart from him. . . . A man scarcely lives at home, a woman scarcely lives outside it. And I need my daughter."

"All right then . . . You see how amenable I am."

"This house will be yours, and Helena's. . . ."

"I appreciate your hospitality. It's something understood between us."

There followed a long discussion in which they arranged everything which concerned their two children's establishment as a family. When it came time to separate, Abel offered Joaquín his hand in a gesture of complete sincerity; he looked at his friend's eyes, and from the depths of his heart cried "Joaquín!" Tears came to the eyes of the doctor as he took the proffered hand.

At the end of a long moment Abel said: "I haven't seen you cry since we were boys, Joaquín."

"We won't see ourselves in that condition again, Abel."

"And that's the worst of it."

And they took leave of each other.

CHAPTER 31

The sun, albeit an autumn sun, seemed to warm Joaquín's cold house following the marriage of his daughter. Joaquín himself seemed to quicken and come alive. He began to transfer his patients to the care of his son-in-law; serious cases he kept under advisement himself, and he let it be known that he acted in a consultative capacity in all matters.

The young Abel, Abelin, using the notes he had gotten from his father-in-law (whom he now called Father, addressing him with the intimate pronoun) and availing himself of the oral help of the doctor, had launched on the compilation of the volume which set forth the medical work of Joaquín Monegro. The youth had approached his subject with a veneration which would not have been possible on the part of the doctor himself. "It is better this way," Joaquín thought, "to have someone else write this account, as Plato did for Socrates." He himself could not, in good conscience and without seeming presumptuous and avid for the unattainable applause of posterity, detail his knowledge and skill. He would reserve his literary energies for other endeavors.

And it was at this point that he began the

serious composition of his *Confession,* the intimate account of his struggle with the passion which consumed his life, the struggle against the demon which had possessed him from the first stirrings of conscience to the present moment. He wrote the account so that after his death his daughter might know of his effort. He addressed the narrative to his daughter; but he was so permeated with the profound tragedy of his life of passion, so self-centered in the story of it, that he entertained the hope that his daughter, or his grandchildren, would one day make the narrative known to the world, to a world which would be seized with both wonder and horror at this darkly afflicted hero who had lived and died in its midst without revealing the depths of his suffering to those around him. For the truth was that Joaquín thought of himself as an exceptional spirit and, as such, more tormented and prone to pain than anyone else, a spirit marked by God with the sign of those predestined to greatness.

My life, dear daughter, has been one long passion, he wrote in the *Confession, and yet I would not have exchanged it for another. I have hated as no one else ever has, for I have felt more than anyone the supreme injustices of the world's favors. The way the parents of your husband acted towards me was neither human nor noble; what they did was infamous; but even worse, much worse, were the acts of every human being upon whom I have relied for love and support since the days of my childhood when I trusted everyone. Why have they rejected me? Why do they prefer the light-headed, the fickle, the egotists? My life has been made bitter by these people. And I have realized that the world is naturally unjust, and that I have not been born among my own. That was my chief misfortune, not to have been born among my own. The vulgarity, the common baseness of those surrounding me, led me to my downfall.*

At the same time that he put together his *Confession,* he was preparing, in case the first effort did not come to fruition, another literary endeavor which would make him eligible to the pantheon of immortals of his people and caste. The second work would be titled *Memoirs of a Doctor,* would be the harvest of a knowledge of the world, of passions, of life, joy and sadness, even of secret crimes, in short, the harvest he had gathered in his years of medical practice. It would be a mirror to life, but revealing the very entrails, the darkest corners of it; a descent into the abysses of human vileness. Into the book he would pour his soul, without speaking of himself; in it, by way of denuding the souls of others, he would denude his own; in it he would take vengeance on the vile world in which he had been forced to exist. When people saw themselves thus exposed and naked they would at first be astounded, but in the end they would admire and respect the author of the exposure; and in it, in this book, he would paint the definitive portraits—their names slightly altered in fictional guise—of Abel and Helena, and these portraits would be the ones to stand for all time. His portrait of that pair would be worth all the portraits Abel would ever paint. And Joaquín savored the satisfaction of knowing that if he were successful in creating this literary portrayal of Abel Sanchez he would immortalize his subject more surely than all Abel's own painting would do, so that critics and commentators in a remote time would discover the actual person of the painter only when they penetrated the thin veil of fiction.

"Yes, Abel," Joaquín told himself, "your best opportunity of attaining what you have so long struggled for, the only thing for which you have striven, the only thing which interests you, for which you denigrated me, and even worse, ignored me, the best chance you have to perpetuate your memory does not lie with your paintings but rather with me, with whether or not I succeed in painting you just as you are, with my pen. And I will succeed, because I know you, because I have withstood you, because you have pressed upon me all my life. I shall unmask you for all time, and you will no longer be Abel

Sanchez, but whatever name I give you. And when you are spoken of as the painter of your paintings, people will say rather: 'Ah, yes, that character of Joaquín Monegro's.' For in that sense you will be my creation, and you will live only as my work lives, and your name will follow along the ground behind me, dragged along in the mud at my heels, as the names of those put in the Inferno were dragged along by Dante. And you will be the perfect symbol of the invidious man."

Of the invidious man! For Joaquín persisted in believing that whatever passion animated Abel beneath his apparently impassive exterior of egotist, whatever feeling moved him was based on envy, his particular type of envy, and that from envy he had usurped, even as a child, the affection of playmates from Joaquín, and from envy had taken Helena from him later. And yet, why then had Abel allowed his own son to be taken away from him? "Ah," Joaquín told himself, "he simply is less concerned with the boy than with the renown of his own name. He doesn't believe in living on in his blood descendants, but only in those who admire his paintings, and he abandons his son to me so he may enjoy fame without competition from someone else with his name. But I shall unmask him."

He was disquieted by his age as he took up the writing of these *Memoirs,* for he had already reached his fifty-fifth year. Still, had not Cervantes begun his *Quixote* in his fifty-seventh year? And he bethought himself of all the other authors who had written their masterpieces after having passed his present age. Moreover, he felt strong, complete master of his mind and will, rich in experience, mature in judgment, his deep feelings and passion—which had been aroused for so many years—subdued and yet ebullient.

Now, in order to complete the work, he would hold himself steadily in check. Poor Abel, what a fate awaited him! He began to feel scorn and compassion for the painter. He looked upon him as a model and as a victim; he studied and observed him carefully, though the opportunity to do so was not very great, for Abel came very seldom to visit his son in his new home.

"Your father must be very busy," Joaquín would say to his son-in-law; "he scarcely appears here. Does he have some complaint against us, I wonder? Have we offended him, Antonia, or my daughter, or I, in some way? I would regret if . . ."

"No, no, Father" (for Abelin now addressed his father-in-law in this manner), "it is nothing of that sort. He doesn't stay at home either. Haven't I told you that he is not interested in anything but his own affairs, and these affairs center around his paintings and whatever . . ."

"No, Son, don't exaggerate, there must be something else."

"No, that's all there is to it."

And, in order to hear the same explanation again, Joaquín would ask the same question again.

"How does it happen," he would ask Helena, "how does it happen Abel doesn't come here?"

"Oh, he is the same about going anyplace!" she would reply. For Helena, on the other hand, did visit her daughter-in-law at her home.

CHAPTER 32

"But tell me," Joaquín said to his son-in-law one day, "why did it never occur to your father to train you in painting, to stir your interest in that direction?"

"I've never cared for it."

"That's beside the point. It would seem natural for him to have wanted to initiate you in his art. . . ."

"On the contrary, he was annoyed whenever I showed any interest in it. He never urged me or encouraged me to do even what other children do as a matter of course, to make drawings and figures."

"That's strange, very strange. And yet . . ."

The young Abel was disturbed by the expression on his father-in-law's face, by the unnatural glare in his eyes. He felt that something writhed within him, something painful which he wished to be rid of, some poisonous secretion. And Joaquín's words were followed by a silence charged with bitterness, a silence which Joaquín broke by saying:

"I simply do not understand why he did not wish to make you into a painter. . . ."

"No, he simply did not want me to be what he was. . . ."

Another silence followed, which Joaquín again suddenly broke, as if with heavy regret and with the air of a man who has decided to make a clean breast of things:

"By heaven, I do understand it!"

Young Abel was shaken, without knowing well why, by the tone with which his father-in-law uttered these words. "Why then . . . ?" he asked.

"No, nothing." Joaquín appeared to have recovered and withdrawn into himself.

"But you must tell me," the youth exclaimed, using the familiar pronoun again, as if addressing a friend—a friend or an accomplice. He was fearful, nevertheless, of hearing what he asked to hear.

"No, no, I don't want you to say later. . . ."

"This way it's worse, Father, than telling me directly, whatever it is. Besides, I think I already know. . . ."

"What . . . ?" Joaquín asked, directing a piercing glance at his son-in-law.

"That he perhaps feared I would some day eclipse him, his own name. . . ."

"Yes," said Joaquín in a wrathful voice, "that's it exactly. Abel Sanchez the son, or Abel Sanchez the Younger—that he could not stand. And that later he should be remembered as your father rather than you remembered as his son. This is a tragedy which has happened more than once within a family. . . . For a son to outshine his father . . ."

"But that is simply . . ." Abel broke off.

"That is simply envy, Son, envy pure and simple."

"Envy of a son! . . . On the part of a father?"

"Yes, and that is the most natural kind. Envy cannot exist between two persons who scarcely know each other. A man from another country or another time is not envied. The outsider, the foreigner is not envied, only the man from the same town; not the man of an older generation, but the contemporary, the comrade. And the greatest envy is between brothers. Witness the legend of Cain and Abel. . . . Certainly the most terrible jealousy is that of a man who thinks his brother desires his wife, the sister-in-law. . . . And then there is the jealousy between fathers and sons. . . ."

"But what of the difference in age in this case?"

"It makes no difference. The fact that a being whom we created should come to obscure our own existence proves too much."

"And between master and disciple, then . . . ?"

Joaquín remained silent. For a moment he fixed his gaze on the floor; then he spoke, as if to the earth beneath his feet:

"Decidedly, envy is a form of family relation." And he added: "But let us talk of something else; and forget all this as if it had never been spoken. Do you hear?"

"No!"

"How do you mean, no?"

"I mean I did not hear what you said before."

"I wish neither of us might have heard it."

CHAPTER 33

Helena was in the habit of going to the home of her daughter-in-law with the purpose of introducing there, into this bourgeois home lacking distinction, a more refined tastefulness, a touch of greater elegance, or so she thought. She took it upon herself to correct, according to her lights, the deficiencies in the education of poor Joaquina, who had been brought up by a father filled with an unreasoning arrogance and an unfortunate mother who had to bear with a man rejected by another woman. And every day she expounded some lesson in manners and smart taste.

"All right, just as you wish." Antonia was always agreeable enough.

Joaquina's reaction was different: though she burned inwardly, she resigned herself; nevertheless, she felt that some day she would rebel; if she restrained herself, it was because of her husband's entreaties.

"It will be as *you* wish, madame," she said once, emphasizing the formal pronoun which they had never ceased to use between them; "I don't understand these matters, nor do they concern me. In all of this, it will be as you please. . . ."

"But it is not as I please, Daughter, but simply a matter of . . ."

"It's all the same! I have been brought up in this house, a doctor's house, and when it's a question of hygiene, of health, or when later the child comes, and it's a question of raising it, I know what must be done; but now, in these niceties which you call matters of taste and refinement I must submit to one who has been formed in the house of an artist."

"But you musn't get yourself into this state. . . ."

"Not at all, it's not that I get into a state. It's simply that you are always throwing it in our faces that what we do should not be done our way but some other way. After all, though, we are not arranging evening parties or tea-dances."

"I don't know where you have picked up this pretended scorn. . . . Yes, pretended, I say it's pretended. . . ."

"I have not said anything to indicate, madame . . ."

"This pretended, this feigned scorn of all good form, of all social convention. A fine fix we would be in without them! . . . It would be utterly impossible to live!"

* * *

Joaquina had been advised by both her father and her husband to take long walks, to expose to the sun and air the flesh and blood which was forming the flesh and blood of the coming child. Since the two men could not always accompany her and Antonia did not like to leave the house, Helena was usually the one to go with her. The mother-in-law was pleased to take these walks, to have Joaquina at her side like a younger sister (which was what people who did not know them took her to be), to overshadow her with the splendid beauty which the years had left intact. Beside her, the daughter-in-law was effaced, and Helena remained the object of the precipitous stares of the passers-by. Joaquina's attraction was of a completely different sort: it was a charm to be relished slowly by the eyes. Helena, on the other hand, dressed herself to dazzle the gaze of anyone who might be distracted. "I'll take the mother!" a passing young gallant provocatively murmured one day at Helena's side as he heard her call Joaquina "Daughter"; the older woman breathed heavier, moistening her lips with the end of her tongue.

"Listen, Daughter," she would tell Joaquina, "you must do your best to hide your condition. It is very unbecoming for a girl to let it be seen that she is pregnant. It looks brazen and ill-humored."

"I'm simply trying to stay as easy and comfortable as possible, and not pay any attention to what people think or don't think. . . . Even though I am in 'an interesting condition,' as affected people and wolves say, I don't pretend I am interesting or interested, in their sense, no matter what other women may have done while in this condition. I am not concerned. . . ."

"Well, you have to be concerned. You live in the world."

"And what difference does it make if people *do* know? . . . Or don't you want them to know, Mother, that you are on your way to becoming a grandmother?"

Helena was piqued both by the insinuation and the thought; but she controlled herself. "Well, listen, as far as age is concerned. . . ."

"Yes, as far as age is concerned, you could be a mother all over again," said Joaquina, wounding the other woman to the quick.

"Yes, of course," said Helena, choked and surprised, disarmed by the sharp attack on her. "But the idea that they should see you. . . ."

"No, you can rest easy on that score, because it's you they look at rather than at me. People remember that wonderful portrait of you, that work of art. . . ."

"Well, if I were in your place . . ." began the mother-in-law.

"You in my place, Mother? And supposing you could join me in this same condition, would you?"

"Look, girl, if you go on in this vein, we will

return to the house at once, and I shall never go out with you again, nor set foot in your house, in your father's house, that is. . . ."

"My house, madame, mine, and my husband's . . . and yours, too!"

"Where in heaven's name have you gotten this temper of yours?"

"Temper, is it? Ah, of course, temperament belongs only to artists."

"Oho, listen to our harmless little mouse, the one who was going to become a nun before her father hooked my son for her. . . ."

"I have already asked you, madame, not to repeat this lie. I know well enough what I did."

"And my son does too."

"Yes, he too knows what he has done. And let's not talk of it again."

CHAPTER 34

And the son of young Abel and Joaquina, in whom was mingled the blood of Abel Sanchez and Joaquín Monegro, was born into the world.

The first battle occurred over the name which should be given the child. The mother wanted the boy to be called Joaquín; Helena wanted his name to be Abel. The decision was left to Joaquín by Abel, by his son Abelin, and by Antonia. A veritable struggle took place thereupon in the soul of Monegro; the simple task of naming a new human being took on for him the character of a fateful augury, a magical determination; it was as if the future of the new spirit were being decided.

"His name should be Joaquín, the same as mine; after a while it would be written Joaquín S. Monegro, and eventually the S. would be left out, the S. which was the only remnant of the Sanchez, and *his* name, his son's name and his entire line would be absorbed into mine. . . . And yet, wouldn't it be better if his name were Abel Monegro, Abel S. Monegro, so that the Abel might be thus redeemed? Abel is his grandfather, but an Abel is also his father, my son-in-law, who now has become the same as a real son to me, my own Abel whom I have created. And what difference does it make if the new child is called Abel, if his other grandfather will not be remembered as Abel but as whatever I call him in my fictional memoirs, by whatever name I brand on his forehead? . . . But then again, . . ."

And while he thus wavered, it was Abel Sanchez the painter who finally decided the issue:

"Let him be called Joaquín. Abel the grandfather, Abel the father, Abel the son, three Abels. . . . It's too many. Besides, I don't like the name; it's the name of a victim. . . ."

"You were glad to give the name to your own son," Helena objected.

"It was your idea, and rather than make any objection . . . But imagine what would have happened if instead of taking up medicine he had become a painter. . . . Abel Sanchez the Elder and Abel Sanchez the Younger. . . ."

"And there cannot be more than one Abel Sanchez," interposed Joaquín, amused to have been proven so completely right in his conjecture.

"As far as I am concerned there could be a hundred of them," replied Abel. "I would always be myself."

"Who could doubt it?" asked his friend.

"An end to it, let him be called Joaquín. It's decided!"

"And let him not take up painting, eh?"

"Nor medicine either," Abel concluded, pretending to follow along with the pretended jest.

And the child was called Joaquín.

CHAPTER 35

The newborn child's grandmother Antonia, who was the one to take care of it, would hug the infant to her breast as if to protect it from some imagined danger and whisper: "Sleep, my child, sleep, for the more you sleep the better, especially in this house, where it is better to be asleep than awake, and you will grow strong and healthy, and let us pray God that the two warring bloods do not quarrel in you; for otherwise what will become of you?"

And the child grew; he grew along with the written pages of the *Confession* and the *Memoirs* of his maternal grandfather, and with the artistic fame of his paternal grandfather. Abel's reputation as a painter was never greater than it now became; and he, for his part, seemed to occupy himself very little with whatever did not deal with this fame.

One morning, when he saw his grandchild sleeping in its cradle, he fixed his gaze on the infant with more than usual intensity and exclaimed: "What a beautiful study this would make!" And taking out a notebook he set about making a pencil sketch of the sleeping child.

"What would you call a finished drawing of

such a subject?" Joaquín asked him. "A study of innocence?"

"The habit of giving titles to paintings is peculiar to the literati; something like the doctors' habit of giving names to diseases they can't cure."

"And whoever told you that the real purpose of medicine was to cure illnesses?"

"What is it then?"

"Knowledge; a knowledge of disease. The end of all science is knowledge."

"I had thought it was knowledge in order to cure. What use otherwise our having tasted the fruit of the knowledge of good and evil, if not to free ourselves of the evil?"

"And the end of art, what is it? What is the end purpose of this sketch you have just made of our grandchild?"

"That is its own end; it contains its purpose. It is an object of beauty and that's enough."

"What is the beautiful object, your sketch or our grandchild?"

"Both of them!"

"Do you perhaps think that your drawing is more beautiful than the little Joaquín?"

"Oh, now you're off on your mania! Joaquín, Joaquín!"

Antonia the grandmother came and took the child from its cradle and carried it off, as if to defend it from each of the grandfathers. Meanwhile she whispered to him: "Ah, my little one, my little one, little lamb of God, sun of this house, angel without blemish, let them leave you alone, neither to draw you or treat you! Don't you be a model for any painter, or a patient for any doctor. . . . Let them have their art and their science, and you come with your grandmother, my little life, my tiny life. You are my life, our life, the sunshine warming this house. I will show you how to pray for your two grandfathers, and God will hear you. Come with me, my little life, lambkin without stain, little lamb of God." And Antonia would not stop to look at, nor did she care to see, Abel's sketch of the child.

CHAPTER 36

Joaquín anxiously followed, with his sickly anxiety, the growth in body and spirit of his grandson Joaquinito. Whom did he take after? Whom did he resemble? Which family was uppermost in him? He watched him all the more anxiously once he began to talk.

Joaquín was disturbed that the other grandfather, Abel, spent more and more time in his house, his son's house, now that the grandchild had been born, and he was amazed that the painter also saw to it that the child was frequently brought to his own home. Abel, that great and grandiose egotist—for such did his own son and his fellow parent-in-law consider him—seemed to have become intensely human, even somewhat like a child himself, in the presence of the newborn. He soon began to make drawings especially for the child, and gradually these began to delight the young Joaquín. "Little grandfather, Abelito, make saints!" And Abel never tired of drawing dogs, cats, horses, bulls, human figures. The child would ask for a horseman one time, two boys boxing another time, a boy running from a dog which ran after, or a repetition of all the previous scenes.

"Never in my life have I been happier to do

something," Abel said. "This is pure pleasure; the rest is nonsense."

"You can put together an album of drawings for the children," Joaquín added.

"No, there would be no charm in that, not for the children. . . . That wouldn't be art, but rather . . ."

"Pedagogy," interposed Joaquín.

"It would be that, whatever else it might be, but certainly not art. This is most like art, these drawings which our grandchild will tear up within half an hour."

"And if I were to save them?"

"Save them? What for?"

"I've heard of a book recently published containing drawings of this type which added greatly to the artist's reputation."

"I'm not making these drawings for publication, do you understand? And as regards reputation, which is one of your great preoccupations, you might as well know that I don't give a fig for it."

"Hypocrite! Why, it's the only thing that really does concern you. . . ."

"The only thing? It doesn't seem possible that you should accuse me of that. What concerns me now is this child; and that he may become a great artist."

"That he may inherit your genius, you mean?"

"And yours too."

The child watched the duel between the two grandfathers without comprehending, although he could guess at something amiss from their attitudes.

"What can be happening to my father," Abel's son asked Joaquín, "that he has become so crazy about his grandson? He never paid me the slightest attention. I don't recall, either, that he ever made me such drawings when I was a child."

"It's simply that we are becoming old," Joaquín answered, "and age teaches one a great deal."

"The other day, when the child asked him some question or other, I even saw him conceal some tears. The first tears I've ever seen from him."

"Oh, that's merely a cardiac reaction."

"How?"

"The truth is that your father is worn by the years and by work, by the effort of artistic endeavor and by his emotions. In short, he has a very weak heart, and any day . . ."

"Any day what?"

"He will give you, that is to say us, a great shock. . . . I am actually glad that the occasion to tell you this has arrived. You might as well prepare your mother too."

"It's true he does complain of fatigue, of dyspnea. . . . Can it be . . . ?"

"Exactly. He has had me examine him without your knowledge, and I have done so. He needs attention."

And thus as soon as the weather began to get raw Abel stayed home and had the grandchild brought to him, a circumstance which embittered the other grandfather's entire day. "He is spoiling the child," Joaquín complained; "and he's trying to steal all his love; he wants to be first in his affection, and make up for his son's affection for me. He is doing it for revenge, yes, for vengeance. He wants to take away this last consolation from me. It's always he, the same one who took away my friend when we were children."

Meanwhile, Abel was instructing the child to love his other grandfather.

"I love you more," the child said to him one time.

"No, no. You mustn't love me more. You must love all of us the same. First, mother and father, and then the grandfathers, and each one the same. Your grandfather Joaquín is a very good man, he loves you very much, he buys you toys. . . ."

"You buy me toys too. . . ."

"He tells you stories. . . ."

"I like your drawings better. Will you make me a bull now, and a picador on horseback?"

CHAPTER 37

One day Joaquín came to see Abel. "Look, Abel," Joaquín said grimly as soon as they were alone, "I've come to talk to you about a serious matter, very serious, a matter of life and death."

"My illness?"

"No. But, if you will, of mine."

"Of yours?"

"Yes, mine. I've come to talk to you about our grandchild. Rather than beat around the bush, let me say that I think you should go away, far enough so that we don't see each other. I pray you, I beg you to do this. . . ."

"I, go away? Are you mad? Why should I go?"

"The child loves you and not me. That's clear. I don't know what you do to him . . . I don't want to know. . . ."

"I bewitch him, no doubt, or give him a potion. . . ."

"I don't know. Some perverse hold. . . . Your drawings are symptomatic. . . ."

"The drawings are evil too, then? You're not well, Joaquín."

"It may be that I am not well, but that no longer matters. I am not at an age to be cured. And if I am unwell, you should make allowances, show me some consideration. . . . Listen,

Abel, you made my youth miserable, you have hounded me all my life long. . . "

"*I* have?"

"Yes, you, you."

"I never knew it, then."

"Don't pretend. You have always despised and denigrated me."

"Look, if you continue in this way, I am leaving the room, because you will make me really ill. You know well enough that I am not in condition to listen to madness of this sort. Go away yourself, go to an institution where they can treat you or take care of you, and leave us alone."

"Abel, for the sole purpose of humiliating me, for the sole purpose of debasing me, you deprived me of Helena, you took her away from me. . . ."

"And haven't you had Antonia?"

"No, it was not for her sake you did it. It was an affront on your part, scorn, mockery. . . ."

"You're not well, Joaquín. I repeat, you are not well."

"You are worse off."

"As regards my body, that's true. I know I have not long to live. . . ."

"Too long."

"Ah, you want my death then?"

Joaquín's manner changed quickly. "No, Abel, no, I didn't say that." And then, with a plaintive note in his voice he added: "But please do go away from here. You can live somewhere else. Leave me the child . . . don't take him away from me . . . for the little time you have left. . . ."

"For the little time I have left then, let him stay with me."

"No, you pervert him with your tricks, you lure him away from me, you alienate him, you teach him to despise me. . . ."

"That's a lie! He has never heard from me, nor ever will, anything disparaging about you."

"It's sufficient that you sway him in some way, that you beguile him."

"And do you think that if I went away, that if I were to step out, he would therefore love you? Even if one wants to, Joaquín, it's impossible with you, it's impossible to love you. . . . You repel everyone, you reject them. . . ."

"You see, you see . . ."

"And if the boy does not love you as you want to be loved, to the exclusion of everyone else or more than anyone else is loved, it's because he senses the danger, because he fears. . . ."

"What does he fear? . . ." hissed Joaquín, turning pale.

"The contagion of your bad blood."

It was then that Joaquín rose, livid with anger. He came at Abel, and his hands went out like two claws for the sick man's throat.

"You thief!" he shrieked.

He had scarce laid hands on the victim before he drew back in horror. Abel gave a cry, clapped his hands to his chest, and murmured, "I'm dying!"

"An angina attack," thought Joaquín, "there's nothing to be done. It's the end!"

At that moment he heard the voice of the grandson calling, "Grandfather, grandfather." Joaquín turned around.

He heard his own voice: "Who are you calling? Which grandfather do you want? . . . Is it me you want?" The child was before him now, but was stricken dumb by the mystery lying there before him. "Come, tell me. Which grandfather were you calling? Was it me?"

The boy at length replied: "No. I was calling grandfather Abel."

"Abel was it? Well there you have him . . . dead. Do you know what that means, dead?"

Almost mechanically Joaquín raised the dead man's head and arranged his body in the armchair in which he had died. Then he turned to his grandson once more; he spoke in an unearthly voice:

"Yes, he's dead. And I killed him. Abel has been killed again by Cain, by your grandfather who is Cain. And now you have the power to kill me if you want. For he wanted to steal you away from me. He wanted to take away all your affections. And he has succeeded. . . . The fault was his." He was weeping now. "He wanted to rob me of you, who were the only consolation left for the poor Cain. Won't they leave Cain anything? Come to me now, and put your arms around me."

The child fled uncomprehending. He fled as if from a madman. And as he fled he called his grandmother Helena.

Alone, Joaquín continued to speak: "I killed him, but he was killing me. For over forty years he has been killing me. He poisoned all the walks of my life with his lording it over me, his triumphs and his celebration. He wanted to steal the child from me. . . ."

On hearing hurried footsteps Joaquín took hold of himself and turned. It was Helena who entered.

"What has happened. . . . What does the child mean? . . ."

"Your husband's sickness has come to a fatal end," said Joaquín coldly.

"You!"

"I was not able to do anything. One is always late in this type of case."

Helena fixed him with steady eyes: "You . . . It was you!"

Then, shaken and white, but maintaining her composure, she went to her dead husband's side.

CHAPTER 38

A year passed during which Joaquín fell into a profound melancholy. He abandoned his *Memoirs,* and avoided seeing anyone, including his children. The death of Abel would have seemed a natural end to his gnawing disease, but a kind of blight had settled upon the house. For her part, Helena found that mourning and black suited her; she set about selling the remaining paintings left by her husband; she also seemed to have developed a certain aversion towards her small grandson. Meanwhile, another child had been born, so that there was now a granddaughter as well.

Joaquín himself was finally brought to bed by the onslaught of some obscure complaint. He felt himself slipping, at the boundary of death, and one day he summoned his family, his son-in-law's, his wife, and Helena.

"The child told you the truth," he blurted out at once, "it was I who killed Abel."

"Don't say such things, Father," his son-in-law pleaded.

"There's no time for either interruptions or falsehoods. I killed him. Or just as well as killed him, for he died in my hands. . . ."

"That's another matter."

"He died when I seized him by the throat. It was all like a dream. My entire life has been a dream. But this was like a nightmare which happens just at the moment of waking, at dawn, between sleep and consciousness. I have not really lived nor slept . . . not even when awake. I no longer remember my parents; I don't want to remember them, and I trust that now that they are long dead, they have forgotten me. . . . And God, too, perhaps will forget me . . . in eternal forgetfulness perhaps there is peace. And you, too, my children, must forget me."

"That is not possible," exclaimed his son-in-law, and he took the doctor's hand and kissed it.

"Don't touch me! These are the hands which were at your father's neck when he died. Don't touch them. . . . But don't leave me yet. . . . Pray for me."

"Father, Father," cried his daughter, unable to say more.

"Why have I been so envious, so bad? What did I do to become that way? What mother's milk did I suck? Was there a philter, a potion of hate mixed with it? A potion in the blood? Why must I have been born into a country of hatreds? Into a land where the precept seems to be: 'Hate thy neighbor as thyself.' For I have lived hating myself; and here we all live hating ourselves. Still . . . bring the child."

"Father!"

"Bring the child!"

When the child was brought, he had him come near: "Do you forgive me?" he asked.

"There is no reason whatever to do so," interrupted Abel.

"Tell him you do," said the child's mother. "Go to your grandfather and tell him you do."

"Yes . . ." whispered the boy.

"Tell me clearly, my child, tell me you forgive me."

"Yes, I do," said the child ingenuously.

"That's it. It's only from you I need forgiveness, from you who have not yet reached the age of reason, who are still innocent. . . . And don't forget your grandfather Abel, who made you drawings. Will you forget him?"

"No!"

"No, don't forget him, my child, don't forget him. . . . And you, Helena. . . ." Her gaze fixed before her, Helena was silent.

"And you, Helena . . ." the dying man repeated.

"I, Joaquín, have forgiven you a long time ago."

"I didn't mean to ask you that. I only wanted to see you next to Antonia. Antonia. . . ."

That poor woman, her eyes swollen with tears, threw herself down on the bed by her husband, as if seeking to protect him.

"It is you, Antonia, who have been the real

victim. You could not cure me, you could not make me good. . . ."

"But you have been, Joaquín. . . . You have suffered so much!"

"Yes, from a phthisis, a tuberculosis of the soul. But you could not make me good because I have not loved you."

"Don't say that!"

"I do say it, I must say it, I say it here before everyone. I have not loved you. If I had loved you I would have been saved. I have not loved you, and now it pains me that this was so. If we could begin all over again. . . ."

"Joaquín, Joaquín!" cried the poor woman from the depths of her broken heart. "Don't say such things. Have pity on me, have pity on your children, on the grandson who is listening to you even though he doesn't seem to understand, . . . perhaps tomorrow. . . ."

"That's why I've said it, out of pity. No, I have not loved you. I haven't wanted to love you. . . . If we were to start all over again! . . . Now, for it's now that . . ."

His wife did not let him finish. She covered his dying mouth with her own, as if she wished to recover his last breath.

"I will save you, this will save you, Joaquín."

"Save me? What do you call salvation?"

"You can still live a few more years, if you want to. . . ."

"What for? So as finally to grow old, really old? No, old age isn't worth it, egotistic old age is no more than a state of infancy with a consciousness of death. An old man is a child who knows he will die. No, no, I don't want to become an old man. I would fight with my grandchildren from pure jealousy, I would grow to hate them. . . . No, no . . . enough of hatred! I could have loved you, I should have loved you, it would have been my salvation, but I did not."

He fell silent. He could not, or did not want to continue. He kissed the members of his family. A few hours later he gave his last weary breath.

THE MADNESS OF DOCTOR MONTARCO

THE MADNESS OF DOCTOR MONTARCO

I first met Dr. Montarco just after his arrival in the city. A secret attraction drew me to him. His appearance was obviously in his favor, and his face had an open and guileless look about it. He was tall, blond, robust, yet quick in movement. He immediately made a friend of everyone he knew, because if he was not to make a person his friend, he refrained from making him his acquaintance. It was difficult to know which of his gestures were natural and which were studied, so subtly had he combined naturalness and art. From this proceeded the fact that while there were some who criticized him for affectation and found his simplicity studied, others of us thought that whatever he did was natural and spontaneous. He himself told me later: "There are gestures which, natural enough to begin with, later become artificial after they have been repeatedly praised. And then there are other gestures which, though we have acquired them after hard work and even against our very nature, end by becoming completely natural and seemingly native to us."

This observation should be enough to show that Dr. Montarco was not, while he was still of sound mind, the extravagant personality which many claimed. Far from it. He was, on the contrary, a man who in conversation expressed discreet and judicious opinions. Only on rare occasions, and even then only with persons completely in his confidence (as I came to be), did he unbridle his feelings and let himself go; it was then he would indulge in vehement invective against the people who surrounded him and from whom he had to gain his livelihood. And thus was prefigured the abyss into which his spirit was finally to fall.

He was one of the most orderly and simple men I have ever known. He was not a "connoisseur" or collector of anything, not even of books, nor did I ever detect in him any monomania whatever. His practice, his home, and his literary work: these were his only preoccupations. He had a wife and two daughters, aged eight and ten, when he arrived in the city. He was preceded by a very good reputation as a doctor; nevertheless, it was no secret that he had been forced by his peculiar conduct to leave his native town. His greatest peculiarity, in the eyes of his medical colleagues, lay in the fact that although he was an excellent practitioner and very well versed in medical science and biology, and that although he was a voluminous writer, it never seemed to occur to him to write about medicine. As he told me once, in his characteristically violent manner: "Why must these idiots insist that I write of professional matters? I studied medicine simply to cure sick people and earn my living doing so. Do I cure them? I do; and therefore let them leave me in peace and spare me their nonsense, and let them keep out of my business. I earn my living as conscientiously as I can, and, once my living is made, I do with my life what I want, and not what these louts want me to do. You can't imagine what profound misery of a moral sort there is in the attempt, which so many people make, to confine everybody to a specialty. For my part, I find a tremendous advantage in living *from* one activity and *for* another. . . . You probably don't need to be reminded of Schopenhauer's justified denunciation of professional philosophers and busybodies."

A little while after arriving in the city, and after he had built up a better than average practice and had acquired the reputation of a serious, careful, painstaking and well-endowed doctor, a local journal published his first story, a story halfway between fantasy and humor, without descriptive writing and without a moral. Two days later I found him very upset; when I asked the reason, he burst forth: "Do you think I'm going to be able to resist the overwhelming pressure of the idiocy prevailing here? Tell me, do you think so? It's the same thing all over again, exactly the same as in my town, the very same! And just as happened there, I'll end by becoming known as a madman. I, who am a marvel of calm. And my patients will gradually drop away, and I'll lose my practice. Then the dismal days will come again, days filled with despair, disgust, and bad temper, and I will have to leave here just as I had to leave my own town."

"But what has happened?" I was finally able to ask.

"What has happened? Simply that five people have already approached me to ask what I meant by writing the piece of fiction I just published, what I intended to say, and what bearing did it have. Idiots, idiots, and thrice idiots! They're worse than children who break dolls to find out what's inside. This town has no hope of salvation, my friend; it's simply condemned to seriousness and silliness, two blood sisters. People here have the souls of school teachers. They believe no one could write except to prove something, or defend or attack some proposition, or from an ulterior motive. One of these blockheads asked me the meaning of my story and by way of reply I asked *him:* 'Did it amuse you?' And he answered: 'As far as that goes, it certainly did; as a matter of fact, I found it quite amusing; but . . .' I left the last word in his mouth, because as soon as he reached this point in the conversation, I turned my back on him and walked away. That a piece of writing is amusing wasn't enough for this monster. They have the souls of school teachers, the souls of school teachers!"

"But, now . . ." I ventured to take up the argument.

"Listen," he interrupted, "don't you come at me with any more 'buts.' Don't bother. The infectious disease, the itch of our Spanish literature is the urge to preach. Everywhere a sermon, and a bad sermon at that. Every little Christ sets himself up to dispense advice, and does it with a poker-face. I remember picking up the *Moral Epistle to Fabian* and being unable to get beyond the first three verses; I simply couldn't stomach it. This breed of men is totally devoid of imagination, and so all their madness is merely silly. An oyster-like breed—there's no use of your denying it—; oysters, that's what they are, nothing but oysters. Everything here savors of oyster beds, or ground-muck. I feel like I'm living among human tubers. And they don't even break through the ground, or lift their heads up, like regular tubers."

In any case, Dr. Montarco did not take heed, and he went and published another story, more satirical and fantastic than the first. I recall Servando Fernández Gómez, a patient of Dr. Montarco, discussing it with me.

"Well sir," said the good Fernández Gómez, "I really don't know what to do now that my doctor has published his stories."

"How is that?" I asked him with some surprise.

"Frankly, it seems rather risky, putting oneself in the hands of a man who writes things like that."

"Come, now, he gives you good care as a doctor, doesn't he?"

"There's no question of that. I've no complaint on that score. Ever since putting myself in his hands, consulting with him and following his regimen, I'm much better and every day I notice a further improvement. Still, those pieces of his . . . he must not be well himself. He sounds as if he had a head full of crickets."

"Don't be alarmed, Don Servando. I have many dealings with him, as you know, and I've observed nothing at all wrong with him. He is a very sensible man."

"When one talks to him he answers appropriately enough and what he says is very sensible, but . . ."

"Listen, I'd rather have a man operate on me who had a steady hand and eye even if he did speak wildly (though Montarco doesn't do that either), than a man who was exquisitely proper, full of sententious wisdom and every kind of platitude and then went ahead and threw my whole body out of joint."

"That may be. Still . . ."

The next day I asked Dr. Montarco about Fernández Gómez, and he responded dryly: "A constitutional fool!"

"What's that?"

"A fool by physiological constitution, *a nativitate,* congenital, irremediable."

"Sounds like the absolute and eternal fool."

"No doubt . . . for, in this area an Absolute fool and a Constitutional one are the same thing; it's not as in politics, where the Absolutists and the Constitutionalists are at opposite poles."

"He says your head must be full of crickets. . . ."

"And his head, and those of his kind, are full of cockroaches. And cockroaches are merely mute crickets. At least mine can sing, or chirrup, or creak out something."

A short time later the doctor published his third tale; and this time the narrative was more pointed, full of ironies, mockery and ill-concealed invective.

"I don't know whether you're doing the wisest thing by publishing these stories," I told him.

"By heaven, I have to. I simply have to express

myself and work off my feelings. If I didn't write out these atrocities I'd end by committing them. I know well enough what I'm doing."

"There are some people who say that all this doesn't suit a man of your age, position, and profession . . ." I said by way of drawing him out.

At this, he jumped to his feet and exclaimed:

"Just as I told you, exactly what I've said a thousand times: I'll have to go away from here, or I shall die of hunger, or they'll drive me crazy, or all of these things together. Yes, that's it, all three at once: I shall have to leave, a madman, to die of hunger. And they talk about my position, do they? What do those blockheads mean by position? Listen, believe me, we shall never emerge from barbarism in Spain, never be more than fancy Moroccans, fancy and false, for we'd be better off being our simple African selves, until we stop insisting that our chief of state be illiterate, that he write not a word, not even a volume of epigrams, or some children's tales, or a farce, while he is in office. He risks his prestige by literacy, they say. Meanwhile, we risk our history and our evolution with the opposite. How stupid and heavy-handed we are!"

Thus impelled by a fatal insight did Dr. Montarco set himself to combat the public sentiment of the city in which he lived and worked. At the same time he strove to be more and more conscientious and meticulous in his professional duties and in his civic and domestic obligations. He took extreme care to attend to his patients in every way, and to study their ills. He greeted everyone with extreme affability; he was rude to no one. In speaking to a person he would choose the topic he thought most likely to interest them, seeking thus to please them. In his private life he continued to be the ideal, the exemplary, husband and father. Still, his tales continued to grow more fanciful and extravagant: such was the opinion of the multitude, who also thought he was straying further and further from the "normal," the "usual." And his patients were beginning to abandon him, creating a void around him. Whereupon his ill-concealed animosity became evident once more.

And this was not the worst of it, for a malicious rumor began to take form and to spread: he was said to be arrogant. Without foundation of any sort, it began to be whispered that the doctor was a haughty spirit, a man concerned only with himself, who gave himself airs and considered himself a genius, while he thought other people poor devils incapable of understanding him. I told him about this consensus and this time, instead of breaking out into one of his customary diatribes, as I had expected, he answered me calmly:

"Haughty and proud am I? No! Only ignorant

people, fools, are ever really haughty; and frankly, I don't consider myself a fool; my type of foolishness doesn't qualify me. If we actually could peer into the depths of each other's conscience like that! I know they think I am disdainful of others, but they are wrong. The truth is merely that I don't have the same opinion of them that they have of themselves. And besides —I might as well tell you what I'm really thinking—what is all this talk about pride and striving for superiority worth anyway? For the truth is, my friend, that when a man tries to get ahead of others he is simply trying to save himself. When a man tries to drown out the names of other men he is merely trying to insure that his own be preserved in the memory of living men, because he knows that posterity is a close-meshed sieve which allows few names to get through to other ages. For instance, have you ever noticed the way a fly-trap works?"

"What do you mean? What kind of a . . . ?"

"One of those bottles filled with water, which in the country are set around to catch flies. The poor flies try to save themselves and, since there is no way out but to climb on the backs of others, and thus navigate on cadavers in those enclosed waters of death, a ferocious struggle takes place to see which one can win out. They do not in the least mean to drown each other; all they are trying to do is to stay afloat. Just so in the struggle for fame, which is a thousand times more terrible than the struggle for bread."

"And the struggle for life," I added, "is the same, too. Darwin . . ."

"Darwin?" he cut me off. "Do you know the book *Biological Problems* by William Henry Rolph?"

"No."

"Well, read it. Read it and you will see that it is not the growth and multiplication of a species which necessitates more food and which leads to such struggle, but rather that it is a tendency toward needing more and more food, an impulse to go beyond the purely necessary, to exceed it, which causes a species to grow and multiply. It is not an instinct toward self-preservation which impels us to action, but rather an instinct toward expansion, toward invasion and encroachment. We don't strive to maintain ourselves only, but to be more than we are already, to be everything. In the strong words of Father Alonso Rodriguez, that great man, we are driven by an 'appetite for the divine.' Yes, an appetite for the divine. 'You will be as gods!': thus it was the Devil tempted our first parents, they say. Whoever doesn't aspire to be more than he is, will not be anything. All or nothing! There is profound meaning in that. Whatever Reason may tell us—that great liar who has invented, for the consolation of failures, the doctrine of the golden mean, the *aurea mediocritas,* the 'neither envied nor envying' and other such nonsense—whatever Reason may tell us—and she is not only a liar but a great whore—in our innermost soul, which we now call the Unconscious, with a capital U, in the depths of our spirit, we know that in order to avoid becoming, sooner or later, nothing, the best course to follow is to attempt to become all.

"The struggle for life, for the more-than-life, rather, is an offensive and not a defensive struggle. . . . In this Rolph is quite right. And I, my friend, do not defend myself; I am never on the defensive, instead I believe in the attack. I don't want a shield, which would only weigh me down and hinder me. I don't want anything but a sword. I would rather deliver fifty blows, and receive ten back, than deliver only ten and not receive any. Attack, attack, and no defense. Let them say what they want about me; I won't hear them, I'll take no notice, I will stop my ears, and if, in spite of my precautions, word of what they say reaches me, I will not answer them. If we had centuries of time to spare, I would sooner be able to convince them that they are fools—and you may imagine the difficulty in doing that—than they would convince me I am mad or over-proud."

"But this purely offensive system of yours, Montarco, my friend . . ." I began.

"Yes, yes," he interrupted me again, "it has its flaws. And even one great danger, and that is that on the day my arm weakens or my sword is blunted they will trample me under their feet, drag me about, and make dust of me. But before that happens they will have already accomplished their purpose: they will have driven me mad."

And so it was to be. I began to suspect it when I heard him talk repeatedly about the character of madness, and to inveigh against reason. In the end, they would succeed in driving him mad.

He persisted in issuing his stories, fictions totally different from anything current at this time and place; and he persisted, simultaneously, in not departing one whit from the reasonable sort of life he outwardly led. His patients continued to leave him. Eventually, dire want made itself felt in his household. Finally, as a culmination to his troubles, he could no longer find a journal or paper to print his contributions, nor did his name make any headway or gain any ground in the republic of letters. It all came to an end when a few of us who were his friends took over responsibility for his wife and daughters, and arranged for him to go into an asylum. His verbal aggression had been growing steadily more pronounced.

I remember as if it were yesterday the first day I visited him in the asylum where he was confined. The director, Dr. Atienza, had been a fellow student of Dr. Montarco and manifested an affection and sympathy for him.

"Well, he is quieter these days, more tranquil than at the beginning," the director told me. "He reads a little, very little; I think it would be unwise to deprive him of reading matter absolutely. Mostly, he reads the *Quixote,* and, if you were to pick up his copy of the book and open it at random, it would almost certainly open to Chapter 32, of the Second Part, where is to be found the reply made by Don Quixote to his critic, the ponderous ecclesiastic who at the table of the duke and duchess severely reprimanded the knight-errant for his mad fancies. If you want, we will go and see him now."

And we did so.

"I am very glad that you've come to call," he exclaimed as soon as he saw me, raising his eyes from the *Quixote,* "I'm glad. I was just thinking and wondering if, despite what Christ tells us in the twenty-second verse of the fifth chapter of St. Matthew, we are ever permitted to make use of the forbidden weapon."

"And what is the forbidden weapon?" I asked him.

" 'Whoever shall call his brother "Fool!" shall be liable to the fires of Gehenna.' You see what a terrible sentence that is. It doesn't say whoever calls him assassin, or thief, or bandit, or swindler, or coward, or whoreson, or cuckold, or liberal; no, it says, whosoever shall call him a 'fool.' That, then, is the forbidden weapon. Everything can be questioned except the intelligence, wit and judgment of other people. When a man takes it into his head to have aspirations, to presume to some special knowledge or talent, it's even more complicated. There have been popes who, because they considered themselves great Latinists, would rather have been condemned as heretics than as poor Latinists guilty of solecisms. And there are weighty cardinals who take greater pride in the purity of their literary style than in being good Christians, and for them orthodoxy is no more than a consequence of literary purity. The forbidden weapon! Just consider the comedy of politics: the participants accuse one another of the ugliest crimes, they charge each other covertly with grave offenses, but they are always careful to call each other eloquent, clever, well-intentioned, talented. . . . For, 'Whosoever shall call his brother a fool, shall be liable to the fires of Gehenna.' Nevertheless, do you know why we make no real progress?"

"Perhaps because we must carry tradition on our backs," I ventured to say.

"No, no. It's simply because it is impossible to convince the fools that they *are* fools. On the day on which fools, that is to say, mankind, become truly convinced that they are just that, fools, on that day progress will have reached its goal. Man is born foolish. . . . And yet whosoever calls his brother a fool shall expose himself to the fires of Gehenna. And expose himself to hellfire he did, that grave clergyman, 'one of those who presume to govern great men's houses, and who, not being nobly born themselves, don't know how to instruct those that are, but would have the liberality of the great measured by the narrowness of their own souls, making those whom they govern stingy, when they pretend to teach them frugality. . . .'"

"Do you see," Dr. Atienza whispered to me, "he knows chapters 31 and 32 of the second part of our book by heart."

"He exposed himself to hellfire, I say," the poor madman went on, "this grave ecclesiastic who came out with the duke and duchess to receive Don Quixote, and who sat down at table with him, face to face while they ate. For, a little while later, furious, stupidly envious, and animated by low passions decked out as high wisdom, this boor charged the duke with responsibility before Our Lord for the actions of this 'good man.' . . . *This good man,* the ridiculous and pompous cleric called Don Quixote, and then went on to call him Mister Fool. Mister Fool!, and he the greatest madman of all time!

But he condemned himself to hellfire for calling him that. And in hell he lies."

"Perhaps he is only in purgatory, for the mercy of God is infinite," I dared to say.

"But the guilt of the grave ecclesiastic—who clearly stands for our country in the book, and nothing else—is an enormous one, really enormous," he continued, ignoring my qualifying suggestion. "That ponderous idiot, a genuine incarnation and representative, if there ever was one, of that section of our population which considers itself cultured, that insufferable pedant, after rising peevishly from table and questioning the good sense of his lord, who was feeding him —though it is doubtful if he did anything to earn his keep,—said: 'Well may fools be mad, when wise men celebrate their madness. Your Grace may remain with this pair, if you please, but for my part, as long as they are in this house, I shall keep to my quarters, and thus save myself the labor of reprehending what I can't mend.' And with that, 'leaving the rest of his dinner behind him, away he flung.' He went away; but not entirely, for he and his like still prowl about, classifying people as sane or mad, and deciding which persons are which. . . . It's scandalous and hypocritical, but these great judges call Don Quixote 'the sublime madman' in public—and another packet of phrases they have heard somewhere—and in private, alone with themselves, they call him Mister Fool. Don Quixote, who, in order to go off in pursuit of an empire, the empire of fame, left Sancho Panza the government of an Island! And what office did Mister Fool keep for himself? Not even a ministry! And after all, why did God create the world? For His greater glory, they say, to make it manifest. And should we do less? . . . Pride! Pride! Diabolic pride! That's the cry of the weak and impotent. Bring them here, all those grave and ponderous gentlemen infected with common sense. . . ."

"Let's leave," Dr. Atienza whispered, "he is getting excited."

We cut short the visit with some excuse or other, and I took leave of my poor friend.

"He has been driven mad," Dr. Atienza said as soon as we were alone. "One of the wisest and sanest men I ever knew, and he has been driven mad."

"Why do you say that?" I asked. "Why driven'?"

"The greatest difference between the sane and the insane," he answered me, "is that the sane, even though they may occasionally have mad thoughts, neither express them nor carry them out, while the insane—unless they are hopeless, in which case they do not think mad thoughts at all—have no power of inhibition, no ability to contain themselves. Who has not thought of carrying out some piece of madness—unless he is a person whose lack of imagination borders on imbecility? But he has known how to control himself. And if he doesn't know, he evolves into a madman or a genius, to a greater or lesser extent of one or the other depending on his form of madness. It is very convenient to speak of 'delusions' in this connection, but any delusion which proves itself to be practical, or which impels us to maintain, advance or intensify life, is just as real an emotion and makes as valid an impression as any which can be registered, in a more precise manner, by the scientific instruments so far invented for the purpose. That necessary store of madness—to give it its plainest name—which is indispensable for any progress, the lack of balance which propels the world of the spirit and without which there would be absolute repose—that is, death—this madness, this imbalance, must be made use of in some way or other. Dr. Montarco used it to create his fantastic narratives, and in doing so he freed himself from it and was able to carry on the very orderly and sensible life which he led. And really, those stories. . . ."

"Ah!" I interrupted, "they are profoundly suggestive, they are rich in surprising points of view. I can read and re-read them because of their freshness, for I find nothing more tedious than to be told something in writing which I have already ruminated. I can always read stories like these, without a moral and without description. I have been thinking of writing a critical study of his work, and I entertain the hope that once the public is put on the right track they will finally see in them what they don't today. The public isn't as slow-witted or disdainful as we sometimes think; their limitation is that they want everything given them already masticated, predigested, and made up into capsules ready to be swallowed. Everyone has enough to do simply making a living and can't take the time to chew on a cud which tastes bitter when it is first put in the mouth. But a worthwhile commentary can bring out the virtues of a writer like Dr. Montarco, in whose work only the letter and not the spirit has so far been apperceived."

"Well, his stories certainly fell on rocky ground," Dr. Atienza resumed. "His very strangeness, which in another country would have attracted readers, scared people away here. At every step of the way and confronted with the simplest things, people surfeited with the most didactic and pedantic junk asked insistently: 'Now what does he mean here, what is this man trying to say in this passage?' And then, you know how his patients all deserted him, despite the fact that he gave them perfect care. People began to call him mad, despite his exemplary life. He was accused of passions which, in spite of appearances, did not really dominate him. His writings were all rejected. And then, when he and his family found themselves in actual need, he gave way to mad talk and acts; and it was this madness which he had previously vented in his writings."

"Madness?" I interrupted.

"No, you're right. It wasn't madness. But, now they have succeeded in making it turn into madness. I have been reading his work since he has been here and I realize now that one of their mistakes was to take him for a man of ideas, a writer of ideas, when fundamentally he is no such thing. His ideas were a point of departure, mere raw material, and had as much importance in his writing as earth used by Velásquez in making the pigments had to do with his painting, or as the type of stone Michelangelo used had to do with his *Moses*. And what would we say of a man who, equipped with a microscope and reagent, went to make an analysis of the marble by way of arriving at a judgment of the *Venus de Milo*? At best, ideas are no more than raw material, as I've already said, for works of art, or philosophy, or for polemics."

"I have always thought so," I said, "but I have found this to be one of the doctrines which meets with the most resistance on the part of the public. I remember that once, in the course of watching a game of chess, I witnessed the most intense drama of which I have ever been spectator. It was a truly terrible spectacle. The players did no more than move the chessmen, and they were limited by the canons of the game and by the chessboard; nevertheless, you can not imagine what intensity of passion there was, what tension of a truly spiritual nature, what flow of vital energy! Those who only followed the progress of the game thought they were attending an everyday match, for the two players certainly played without great skill. For my part I was watching the way they picked out the chessmen and played them; I was attentive to the solemn silence, the frowns on the players brows. There was one move, one of the most ordinary and undistinguished no doubt, a check which did not eventuate in a checkmate, which was nevertheless most extraordinary. You should have seen how the one player grasped his knight with his whole hand and placed him on the board with a rap, and how he exclaimed 'Check!' And those two passed for two commonplace players! Commonplace? I'm certain that Morphy or Philidor were more so. . . . Poor Montarco!"

"Yes, poor Montarco! And today you have heard him speak more or less reasonably. . . . Rarely, only rarely, does he talk complete extravagance. When he does, he imagines he is a grotesque character whom he calls the Privy

Counsellor Herr Schmarotzender; he puts on a wig which he has found somewhere, gets up on a chair, and makes a wild speech,—full of spirit, however, and in words which somehow echo all the longing and eternal seeking of humanity. At the end, he gets down and asks me: 'Don't you think, Atienza, my friend, that there is a good deal of truth, basically, in the ravings of the poor Privy Counsellor Herr Schmarotzender?' And, in fact, it often strikes me that the feeling of veneration accorded madmen in certain countries is quite justified."

"You know, it seems to me that you should give up the management of this place."

"Don't concern yourself, my friend. It's not that I believe that the veil of a superior world, a world hidden from us, is lifted for these unfortunates; it's simply that I think they say things we all think but don't dare express because of timidity or shame. Reason, which we have acquired in the struggle for life and which is a conservative force, tolerates only what serves to conserve or affirm this life. We don't understand anything but what we must understand in order to live. But who can say that the inextinguishable longing to survive, the thirst for immortality, is not the proof, the revelation of another world, a world which envelops, and also makes possible, our world? And who can say that when reason and its chains have been broken, such dreams and delirium, such frenzied outbursts as Dr. Montarco's, are not desperate leaps by the spirit to reach this other world?"

"It seems to me, and you will forgive my bluntness in saying so, that instead of your treating Dr. Montarco, Dr. Montarco is treating you. The speeches of the Privy Counsellor are beginning to affect you adversely."

"It may be. The only thing I am sure of is that every day I immure myself deeper in this asylum; for I would rather watch over madmen, than have to put up with fools. The only trouble, really, is that there are many madmen who are also fools. But now I have Dr. Montarco to devote myself to. Poor Montarco!"

"Poor Spain!" I said. I extended my hand and we parted.

Dr. Montarco did not last long in the asylum. He was gradually overcome by a profound melancholy, a crushing depression, and finally sank into an obstinate state of muteness. He emerged from his silence only to murmur: "All or nothing. . . . All or nothing. . . . All or nothing. . . ." His illness deepened and ended in death.

After his death, the drawer to his desk yielded a bulky manuscript whose title page read:

ALL OR NOTHING

I request that on my death this manuscript be burned without being read.

I don't know whether Dr. Atienza resisted the temptation to read it; or whether, in compliance with the madman's last wish, he burned it.

Poor Dr. Montarco! May he rest in peace, for he deserved both peace and final rest.

SAN MANUEL BUENO. MARTYR

SAN MANUEL BUENO, MARTYR

> If with this life only in view we have had hope in Christ, we are of all men the most to be pitied. Saint Paul: I COR. 15:19.

Now that the bishop of the diocese of Renada, to which this my beloved village of Valverde de Lucerna belongs, is seeking (according to rumor), to initiate the process of beautification of our Don Manuel, or more correctly, San Manuel Bueno, who was parish priest here, I want to state in writing, by way of confession (although to what end only God, and not I can say), all that I can vouch for and remember of that matriarchal man who pervaded the most secret life of my soul, who was my true spiritual father, the father of my spirit, the spirit of myself, Angela Carballino.

The other, my flesh-and-blood temporal father, I scarcely knew, for he died when I was still a very young girl. I know that he came to Valverde de Lucerna from the outside world—that he was a stranger—and that he settled here when he married my mother. He had brought a number of books with him: *Don Quixote,* some plays from the classic theatre, some novels, a few histories, the *Bertoldo,* everything all mixed together. From these books (practically the only ones in the entire village), I nurtured dreams as a young girl, dreams which in turn devoured me. My good mother gave me very little account either of the words or the deeds of my father. For the words and deeds of Don Manuel, whom she worshipped, of whom she was enamored, in common with all the rest of the village—in an exquisitely chaste manner, of course—had obliterated the memory of the words and deeds of her husband; him she commended to God, with full fervor, as she said her daily rosary.

Don Manuel I remember as if it were yesterday, from the time when I was a girl of ten, just before I was taken to the convent school in the cathedral city of Renada. At that time Don Manuel, our saint, must have been about thirty-seven years old. He was tall, slender, erect; he carried himself the way our Buitre Peak carries its crest, and his eyes had all the blue depth of our lake. As he walked he commanded all eyes, and not only the eyes but the hearts of all; gazing round at us he seemed to look through our flesh as through glass and penetrate our hearts. We all of us loved him, especially the children. And the things he said to us! Not words, things! The villagers could scent the odor of sanctity, they were intoxicated with it.

It was at this time that my brother Lazarus, who was in America, from where he regularly sent us money with which we lived in decent leisure, had my mother send me to the convent school, so that my education might be completed outside the village; he suggested this move despite the fact that he had no special fondness for the nuns. "But since, as far as I know," he wrote us, "there are no lay schools there yet,—especially not for young ladies—we will have to make use of the ones that do exist. The important thing is for Angelita to receive some polish and not be forced to continue among village girls." And so I entered the convent school. At one point I even thought I would become a teacher; but pedagogy soon palled upon me.

At school I met girls from the city and I made friends with some of them. But I still kept in touch with people in our village, and I received frequent reports and sometimes a visit.

And the fame of the parish priest reached as far as the school, for he was beginning to be talked of in the cathedral city. The nuns never tired of asking me about him.

Ever since early youth I had been endowed, I don't very well know from where, with a large degree of curiosity and restlessness, due at least in part to that jumble of books which my father had collected, and these qualities were stimulated at school, especially in the course of a relationship which I developed with a girl friend, who grew excessively attached to me. At times she proposed that we enter the same convent together, swearing to an everlasting "sisterhood"—and even that we seal the oath in blood. At other times she talked to me, with eyes half closed, of sweethearts and marriage adventures. Strangely enough, I have never heard of her since, or of what became of her, despite the fact that whenever our Don Manuel was spoken of, or when my mother wrote me something about him in her letters—which happened in almost every letter—and I read it to her, this girl would exclaim, as if in rapture: "What luck, my dear, to be able to live near a saint like that, a live saint, of flesh and blood, and to be able to kiss his hand; when you go back to your village write me everything, everything, and tell me about him."

Five years passed at school, five years which now have evanesced in memory like a dream at dawn, and when I became fifteen I returned to my own Valverde de Lucerna. By now everything revolved around Don Manuel: Don

Manuel, the lake and the mountain. I arrived home anxious to know him, to place myself under his protection, and hopeful he would set me on my path in life.

It was rumored that he had entered the seminary to become a priest so that he might thus look after the sons of a sister recently widowed and provide for them in place of their father; that in the seminary his keen mind and his talents had distinguished him and that he had subsequently turned down opportunities for a brilliant career in the church because he wanted to remain exclusively a part of his Valverde de Lucerna, of his remote village which lay like a brooch between the lake and the mountain reflected in it.

How he did love his people! His life consisted in salvaging wrecked marriages, in forcing unruly sons to submit to their parents, or reconciling parents to their sons, and, above all, of consoling the embittered and the weary in spirit; meanwhile he helped everyone to die well.

I recall, among other incidents, the occasion when the unfortunate daughter of old aunt Rabona returned to our town. She had been in the city and lost her virtue there; now she returned unmarried and castoff, and she brought back a little son. Don Manuel did not rest until he had persuaded an old sweetheart, Perote by name, to marry the poor girl and, moreover, to legitimize the little creature with his own name. Don Manuel told Perote:

"Come now, give this poor waif a father, for he hasn't got one except in heaven."

"But, Don Manuel, it's not my fault . . . !"

"Who knows, my son, who knows . . . ! And besides, it's not a question of guilt."

And today, poor Perote, inspired on that occasion to saintliness by Don Manuel, and now a paralytic and invalid, has for staff and consolation of his life the son he accepted as his own when the boy was not his at all.

On Midsummer's Night, the shortest night of the year, it was a local custom here (and still is) for all the old crones, and a few old men, who thought they were possessed or bewitched (hysterics they were, for the most part, or in some cases epileptics) to flock to the lake. Don Manuel undertook to fulfill the same function as the lake, to serve as a pool of healing, to treat his charges and even, if possible, to cure them. And such was the effect of his presence, of his gaze, and above all of his voice—the miracle of his voice!—and the infinitely sweet authority of his words, that he actually did achieve some remarkable cures. Whereupon his fame increased, drawing all the sick of the environs to our lake and our priest. And yet once when a mother came to ask for a miracle in behalf of her son, he answered her with a sad smile:

"Ah, but I don't have my bishop's permission to perform miracles."

He was particularly interested in seeing that all the villagers kept themselves clean. If he chanced upon someone with a torn garment he would send him to the church: "Go and see the sacristan, and let him mend that tear." The sacristan was a tailor, and when, on the first day of the year, everyone went to congratulate him on his saint's day—his holy patron was Our Lord Jesus Himself—it was by Don Manuel's wish that everyone appeared in a new shirt, and those that had none received the present of a new one from Don Manuel himself.

He treated everyone with the greatest kindness; if he favored anyone, it was the most unfortunate, and especially those who rebelled. There was a congenital idiot in the village, the fool Blasillo, and it was toward him that Don Manuel chose to show the greatest love and concern; as a consequence he succeeded in miraculously teaching him things which had appeared beyond the idiot's comprehension. The fact was that the embers of understanding feebly glowing in the idiot were kindled whenever, like a pitiable monkey, he imitated his Don Manuel.

The marvel of the man was his voice; a divine voice which brought one close to weeping. Whenever he officiated at Solemn High Mass and intoned the prelude, a tremor ran through the congregation and all within sound of his voice were moved to the depths of their being. The sound of his chanting, overflowing the church, went on to float over the lake and settle at the foot of the mountain. And when on Good Friday he intoned "My God, my God, my God, why hast Thou forsaken me?" a profound shudder swept through the multitude, like the lash of a northeaster across the waters of the lake. It was as if these people heard the Lord Jesus Christ himself, as if the voice sprang from the ancient crucifix, at the foot of which generations of mothers had offered up their sorrows. And it happened that on one occasion his mother heard him and was unable to contain herself, and cried out to him right in the church, "My son!," calling her child. And the entire congregation was visibly affected. It was as if the mother's cry had issued from the half-open lips of the Mater Dolorosa—her heart transfixed by seven swords—which stood in one of the chapels of the nave. Afterwards, the fool Blasillo went about piteously repeating, as if he were an echo, "My God, my God, my God, why hast Thou forsaken me?" with such effect that everyone who heard him was moved to tears, to the great satisfaction of the fool, who prided himself on this triumph of imitation.

The priest's effect on people was such that no one ever dared to tell him a lie, and everyone confessed themselves to him without need of a confessional. So true was this that on one occasion, when a revolting crime had been committed in a neighboring village, the judge—a dull fellow who badly misunderstood Don Manuel—called on the priest and said:

"Let us see, Don Manuel, if you can get this bandit to admit the truth."

"So that afterwards you may punish him?" asked the saintly man. "No, Judge, no; I will not extract from any man a truth which could be the death of him. That is a matter between him and his God. . . . Human justice is none of my affair. 'Judge not that ye be not judged,' said our Lord."

"But the fact is, Father, that I, a judge . . ."

"I understand. You, Judge, must render unto Caesar that which is Caesar's, while I shall render unto God that which is God's."

And, as Don Manuel departed, he gazed at the suspected criminal and said:

"Make sure, only, that God forgives you, for that is all that matters."

Everyone went to Mass in the village, even if it were only to hear him and see him at the altar, where he appeared to be transfigured, his countenance lit from within. He introduced one holy practice to the popular cult; it consisted in assembling the whole town inside the church, men and women, ancients and youths, some thousand persons; there we recited the Creed, in unison, so that it sounded like a single voice: "I believe in God, the Almighty Father, Creator of heaven and earth . . ." and all the rest. It was not a chorus, but a single voice, a simple united voice, all the voices based on one on which they formed a kind of mountain, whose peak, lost at times in the clouds, was Don Manuel. As we reached the section "I believe in the resurrection of the flesh and life everlasting," the voice of Don Manuel was submerged, drowned in the voice of the populace as in a lake. In truth, he was silent. And I could hear the bells of that city which is said hereabouts to be at the bottom of the lake—bells which are also said to be audible on Midsummer's Night—the bells of the city which is submerged in the spiritual lake of our populace; I was hearing the voice of our dead, resurrected in us by the communion of saints. Later, when I had learned the secret of our saint, I understood that it was as if a caravan crossing the desert lost its leader as they approached the goal of their trek, whereupon his people lifted him on their shoulders to bring his lifeless body into the promised land.

When it came to dying themselves, most of the villagers refused to die unless they were holding on to Don Manuel's hand, as if to an anchor chain.

In his sermons he never inveighed against unbelievers, Masons, liberals or heretics. What for, when there were none in the village? Nor did it occur to him to speak against the wickedness of the press. On the other hand, one of his most frequent themes was gossip, against which he lashed out.

"Envy," he liked to repeat, "envy is nurtured by those who prefer to think they are envied, and most persecutions are the result of a persecution complex rather than of an impulse to persecute."

"But Don Manuel, just listen to what that fellow was trying to tell me . . ."

"We should concern ourselves less with what people are trying to tell us than with what they tell us without trying . . ."

His life was active rather than contemplative, and he constantly fled from idleness, even from leisure. Whenever he heard it said that idleness was the mother of all the vices, he added: "And also of the greatest vice of them all, which is to think idly." Once I asked him what he meant and he answered: "Thinking idly is thinking as a substitute for doing, or thinking too much about what is already done instead of about what must be done. What's done is done and over with, and one must go on to something else, for there is nothing worse than remorse without possible relief." Action! Action! Even in those early days I had already begun to realize that Don Manuel fled from being left to think in solitude, and I guessed that some obsession haunted him.

And so it was that he was always occupied, sometimes even occupied in searching for occupations. He wrote very little on his own, so that he scarcely left us anything in writing, even notes; on the other hand, he acted as scrivener for everyone else, especially mothers, for whom he composed letters to their absent sons.

He also worked with his hands, pitching in to help with some of the village tasks. At threshing time he reported to the threshing floor to flair and winnow, meanwhile teaching and entertaining the workers by turn. Sometimes he took the place of a worker who had fallen sick. One day in the dead of winter he came upon a child, shivering with the bitter cold. The child's father had sent him into the woods to bring back a strayed calf.

"Listen," he said to the child, "you go home and get warm, and tell your father that I am bringing back the calf." On the way back with the animal he ran into the father, who had come out to meet him, thoroughly ashamed of himself.

In winter he chopped wood for the poor. When a certain magnificent walnut tree died—"that matriarchal walnut," he called it, a tree under whose shade he had played as a boy and whose fruit he had eaten for so many years—he asked for the trunk, carried it to his house and, after he had cut six planks from it, which he put away at the foot of his bed, he made firewood of the rest to warm the poor. He also was in the habit of making handballs for the boys and a goodly number of toys for the younger children.

Often he used to accompany the doctor on his rounds, adding his presence and prestige to the doctor's prescriptions. Most of all he was interested in maternity cases and the care of children; it was his opinion that the old wives' sayings "from the cradle to heaven" and the other one about "little angels belong in heaven" were nothing short of blasphemy.[1] The death of a child moved him deeply.

"A child stillborn," I once heard him say, "or one who dies soon after birth, is the most terrible of mysteries to me. It's as if it were a suicide. Or as if the child were crucified."

And once, when a man had taken his own life and the father of the suicide, an outsider, asked Don Manuel if his son could be buried in consecrated ground, the priest answered:

"Most certainly, for at the last moment, in the very last throes, he must certainly have repented. There is no doubt of it whatsoever in my mind."

From time to time he would visit the local school to help the teacher, to teach alongside

1. "Teta y gloria" and "angelitos al cielo."

him—and not only the catechism. The simple truth was that he fled relentlessly from idleness and from solitude. He went so far in this desire of his to mingle with the villagers, especially the youth and the children, that he even attended the village dances. And more than once he played the drum to keep time for the young men and women dancing; this kind of activity, which in another priest would have seemed like a grotesque mockery of his calling, in him somehow took on the appearance of a holy and religious exercise. When the Angelus would ring out, he would put down the drum and sticks, take off his hat (all the others doing the same) and pray: "The angel of the Lord declared unto Mary: Hail Mary . . ." And afterwards: "Now, let us rest until tomorrow."

"First of all," he would say, "the village must be happy; everyone must be happy to be alive. To be satisfied with life is of first importance. No one should want to die until it is God's will."

"I want to die now," a recently widowed woman once told him, "I want to be with my husband . . ."

"And why now?" he asked. "Stay here and pray God for his soul."

One of his well-loved remarks was made at a wedding: "Ah, if I could only change all the water in our lake into wine, into a dear little wine which, no matter how much of it one drank, would always make one joyful without intoxicating . . . or, if intoxicating, would make one joyfully drunk."

Once upon a time a band of poor acrobats came through the village. The leader—who arrived on the scene with a gravely ill and pregnant wife and three sons to help him—played the clown. While he was in the village square making all the children, and even some of the adults, laugh with glee, his wife suddenly fell desperately ill and had to leave; she went off accompanied by a look of anguish from the clown and a howl of laughter from the children. Don Manuel hurried after, and, a little later, in a corner of the inn's stable, he helped her give up her soul in a state of grace. When the performance was over and the villagers and the clown learned of the tragedy, they came to the inn, and there the poor bereaved clown, in a voice choked with tears, told Don Manuel, as he took his hand and kissed it: "They are quite right, Father, when they say you are a saint." Don Manuel took the clown's hand in his and replied before everyone:

"It's you who are the saint, good clown. I watched you at your work and understood that you do it not only to provide bread for your children, but also to give joy to the children of others. And I tell you now that your wife, the mother of your children, whom I sent to God while you worked to give joy, is at rest in the Lord, and that you will join her there, and that the angels, whom you will make laugh with happiness in heaven, will reward you with their laughter."

And everyone present wept, children and elders alike, as much from sorrow as from a mysterious joy in which all sorrow was drowned. Later, recalling that solemn hour, I have come to realize that the imperturbable joyousness of Don Manuel was merely the temporal, earthly form of an infinite, eternal sadness which the priest concealed from the eyes and ears of the world with heroic saintliness.

His constant activity, his ceaseless intervention in the tasks and diversions of everyone, had the appearance, in short, of a flight from himself, of a flight from solitude. He confirmed this suspicion: "I have a fear of solitude," he would say. And still, from time to time he would go off by himself, along the shores of the lake, to the ruins of the abbey where the souls of pious Cistercians seem still to repose, although history has long since buried them in oblivion. There, the cell of the so-called Father-Captain can still be found, and it is said that the drops of blood spattered on the walls as he flagellated himself can still be seen. What thoughts occupied our Don Manuel as he walked there? I remember a conversation we held once in which I asked him, as he was speaking of the abbey, why it had never occurred to him to enter a monastery, and he answered me:

"It is not at all because of the fact that my sister is a widow and I have her children and herself to support—for God looks after the poor—but rather because I simply was not born to be a hermit, an anchorite; the solitude would crush my soul; and, as far as a monastery is concerned, my monastery is Valverde de Lucerna. I was not meant to live alone, or die alone. I was meant to live for my village, and die for it too. How should I save my soul if I were not to save the soul of my village as well?"

"But there have been saints who were hermits, solitaries . . ." I said.

"Yes, the Lord gave them the grace of solitude which He has denied me, and I must resign myself. I must not throw away my village to win my soul. God made me that way. I would not be able to resist the temptations of the desert. I would not be able, alone, to carry the cross of birth . . ."

I have summoned up all these recollections, from which my faith was fed, in order to portray our Don Manuel as he was when I, a young girl of sixteen, returned from the convent of Renada to our "monastery of Valverde de Lucerna," once more to kneel at the feet of our "abbot."

"Well, here is the daughter of Simona," he said as soon as he saw me, "made into a young woman, and knowing French, and how to play the piano, and embroider, and heaven knows what else besides! Now you must get ready to give us a family. And your brother Lazarus; when does he return? Is he still in the New World?"

"Yes, Father, he is still in the New World."

"The New World! And we in the Old. Well then, when you write him, tell him for me, on behalf of the parish priest, that I should like to know when he is returning from the New World to the Old, to bring us the latest from over there. And tell him that he will find the lake and the mountain as he left them."

When I first went to him for confession, I became so confused that I could not enunciate a word. I recited the "Forgive me, Father, for I have sinned," in a stammer, almost a sob. And he, observing this, said:

"Good heavens, my dear, what are you afraid of, or of whom are you afraid? Certainly you're not trembling now under the weight of your sins, nor in fear of God. No, you're trembling because of me, isn't that so?"

At this point I burst into tears.

"What have they been telling you about me? What fairy tales? Was it your mother, perhaps?

Come, come, please be calm; you must imagine you are talking to your brother . . ."

At this I plucked up courage and began to tell him of my anxieties, doubts and sorrows.

"Bah! Where did you read all this, Miss Intellectual. All this is literary nonsense. Don't succumb to everything you read just yet, not even to Saint Theresa. If you need to amuse yourself, read the *Bertoldo,* as your father before you did."

I came away from my first confession to that holy man deeply consoled. The initial fear—simple fright more than respect—with which I had approached him, turned into a profound pity. I was at that time a very young woman, almost a girl still; and yet, I was beginning to be a woman, in my innermost being I felt the juice and stirrings of maternity, and when I found myself in the confessional at the side of the saintly priest, I sensed a kind of unspoken confession on his part in the soft murmur of his voice. And I remembered how when he had intoned in the church the words of Jesus Christ: "My God, my God, why hast Thou forsaken me?" his own mother had cried out in the congregation: "My son!"; and I could hear the cry that had rent the silence of the temple. And I went to him again for confession—and to comfort him.

Another time in the confessional I told him of a doubt which assailed me, and he responded:

"As to that, you know what the catechism says. Don't question me about it, for I am ignorant; in Holy Mother Church there are learned doctors of theology who will know how to answer you."

"But you are the learned doctor here."

"Me? A learned doctor? Not even in thought! I, my little doctress, am only a poor country priest. And those questions, . . . do you know who whispers them into your ear? Well . . . the Devil does!"

Then, making bold, I asked him point-blank:

"And suppose he were to whisper these questions to you?"

"Who? To me? The Devil? No, we don't even know each other, my daughter, we haven't met at all."

"But if he did whisper them? . . ."

"I wouldn't pay any attention. And that's enough of that; let's get on, for there are some people, really sick people, waiting for me."

I went away thinking, I don't know why, that our Don Manuel, so famous for curing the bedeviled, didn't really even believe in the Devil. As I started home, I ran into the fool Blasillo, who had probably been hovering around outside; as soon as he saw me, and by way of treating me to a display of his virtuosity, he began the business of repeating—and in what a manner!—'My God, my God, why hast Thou forsaken me?" I arrived home utterly saddened and locked myself in my room to cry, until finally my mother arrived.

"With all these confessions, Angelita, you will end by going off to a nunnery."

"Don't worry, Mother," I answered her. "I have plenty to do here, in the village, and it will be my only convent."

"Until you marry."

"I don't intend to," I rejoined.

The next time I saw Don Manuel I asked him, looking straight into his eyes:

"Is there really a Hell, Don Manuel?"

And he, without altering his expression, answered:

"For you, my daughter, no."

"For others, then?"

"Does it matter to you, if you are not to go there?"

"It matters for the others, in any case. Is there a Hell?"

"Believe in Heaven, the Heaven we can see. Look at it there"—and he pointed to the heavens above the mountain, and then down into the lake, to the reflection.

"But we are supposed to believe in Hell as well as in Heaven," I said.

"That's true. We must believe everything believed and taught by our Holy Mother Church,

Catholic, Apostolic, and Roman. And now, that will do!"

I thought I read a deep unknown sadness in his eyes, eyes which were as blue as the waters of the lake.

Those years passed as if in a dream. Within me, a reflected image of Don Manuel was unconsciously taking form. He was an ordinary enough man in many ways, of such daily use as the daily bread we asked for in our Paternoster. I helped him whenever I could with his tasks, visiting the sick, his sick, the girls at school, and helping, too, with the church linen and the vestments; I served in the role, as he said, of his deaconess. Once I was invited to the city for a few days by a school friend, but I had to hurry home, for the city stifled me—something was missing, I was thirsty for a sight of the waters of the lake, hungry for a sight of the peaks of the mountain; and even more, I missed my Don Manuel, as if his absence called to me, as if he were endangered by my being so far away, as if he were in need of me. I began to feel a kind of maternal affection for my spiritual father; I longed to help him bear the cross of birth.

My twenty-fourth birthday was approaching when my brother Lazarus came back from America with the small fortune he had saved up.

He came back to Valverde de Lucerna with the intention of taking me and my mother to live in a city, perhaps even Madrid.

"In the country," he said, "in these villages, a person becomes stupefied, brutalized and spiritually impoverished." And he added: "Civilization is the very opposite of everything countryfied. The idiocy of village life! No, that's not for us; I didn't have you sent away to school so that later you might spoil here, among these ignorant peasants."

I said nothing, though I was disposed to resist emigration. But our mother, already past sixty, took a firm stand from the start: "Change pastures at my age?" she demanded at once. A little later she made it quite clear that she could not live out of sight of her lake, her mountain, and, above all, of her Don Manuel.

"The two of you are like those cats that get attached to houses," my brother muttered.

When he realized the complete sway exercised over the entire village—especially over my mother and myself—by the saintly priest, my brother began to resent him. He saw in this situation an example of the obscurantist theocracy which, according to him, smothered Spain. And he commenced to spout the old anti-clerical commonplaces, to which he added anti-religious and "progressive" propaganda brought back from the New World.

"In the Spain of sloth and flabby useless men, the priests manipulate the women, and the women manipulate the men. Not to mention the idiocy of the country, and this feudal backwater!"

"Feudal," to him, meant something frightful. "Feudal" and "medieval" were the epithets he employed to condemn something completely.

The failure of his diatribes to move us and their total lack of effect upon the village—where they were listened to with respectful indifference—disconcerted him no end. "The man does not exist who could move these clods." But, he soon began to understand—for he was an intelligent man, and therefore a good one—the kind of influence exercised over the village by Don Manuel, and he came to appreciate the effect of the priest's work in the village.

"This priest is not like the others," he announced. "He is, in fact, a saint."

"How do you know what the others are like," I asked. To which he answered:

"I can imagine."

In any case, he did not set foot inside the church nor did he miss an opportunity to parade his incredulity—though he always exempted Don Manuel from his scorning accusations. In the village, an unconscious expectancy began to build up, the anticipation of a kind of duel between my brother Lazarus and

Don Manuel—in short, it was expected that Don Manuel would convert my brother. No one doubted but that in the end the priest would bring him into the fold. On his side, Lazarus was eager (he told me so himself, later) to go and hear Don Manuel, to see and hear him in the church, to get to know him and to talk with him, so that he might learn the secret of his spiritual hold over our souls. And he let himself be coaxed to this end, so that finally—"out of curiosity," as he said—he went to hear the preacher.

"Now, this is something else again," he told me as soon as he came from hearing Don Manuel for the first time. "He's not like the others; still, he doesn't fool me, he's too intelligent to believe everything he must teach."

"You mean you think he's a hypocrite?"

"A hypocrite . . . no! But he has a job by which he must live."

As for me, my brother undertook to see that I read the books he brought me, and others which he urged me to buy.

"So your brother Lazarus wants you to read," Don Manuel queried. "Well, read, my daughter, read and make him happy by doing so. I know you will read only worthy books. Read even if only novels; they are as good as the books which deal with so-called 'reality.' You are better off reading than concerning yourself with village gossip and old wives' tales. Above all, though, you will do well to read devotional books which will bring you contentment in life, a quiet, gentle contentment, and peace."

And he, did he enjoy such contentment?

It was about this time that our mother fell mortally sick and died. In her last days her one wish was that Don Manuel should convert Lazarus, whom she expected to see again in heaven, in some little corner among the stars from where they could see the lake and the mountain of Valverde de Lucerna. She felt she was going there now, to see God.

"You are not going anywhere," Don Manuel would tell her; "you are staying right here. Your body will remain here, in this land, and your soul also, in this house, watching and listening to your children though they do not see or hear you."

"But, Father," she said, "I am going to see God."

"God, my daughter, is all around us, and you will see Him from here, right from here. And all of us in Him, and He in all of us."

"God bless you," I whispered to him.

"The peace in which your mother dies will be her eternal life," he told me.

And, turning to my brother Lazarus: "Her heaven is to go on seeing you, and it is at this moment that she must be saved. Tell her you will pray for her."

"But—"

"But what? . . . Tell her you will pray for her, to whom you owe your life. And I know that once you promise her, you *will* pray, and I know that once you pray . . ."

My brother, his eyes filled with tears, drew near our dying mother and gave her his solemn promise to pray for her.

"And I, in heaven, will pray for you, for all of you," my mother responded. And then, kissing the crucifix and fixing her eyes on Don Manuel, she gave up her soul to God.

"Into Thy hands I commend my spirit," prayed the priest.

My brother and I stayed on in the house alone. What had happened at the time of my mother's death had established a bond between Lazarus and Don Manuel. The latter seemed even to neglect some of his charges, his patients and his other needy to look after my brother. In the afternoons, they would go for a stroll together, walking along the lake or toward the ruins, overgrown with ivy, of the old Cistercian abbey.

"He's an extraordinary man," Lazarus told me. "You know the story they tell of how there is a city at the bottom of the lake, submerged beneath the water, and that on Midsummer's Night at midnight the sound of its church bells can be heard . . ."

"Yes, a city 'feudal and medieval' . . ."

"And I believe," he went on, "that at the bottom of Don Manuel's soul there is a city, submerged and inundated, and that sometimes the sound of its bells can be heard . . ."

"Yes . . . And this city submerged in Don Manuel's soul, and perhaps—why not?—in yours as well, is certainly the cemetery of the souls of our ancestors, the ancestors of our Valverde de Lucerna . . . 'feudal and medieval'!"

In the end, my brother began going to Mass. He went regularly to hear Don Manuel. When it became known that he was prepared to comply with his annual duty of receiving Communion, that he would receive when the others received, an intimate joy ran through the town, which felt that by this act he was restored to his people. The rejoicing was of such nature, moreover, so openhanded and honest, that Lazarus never did feel that he had been "vanquished" or "overcome."

The day of his Communion arrived; of Communion before the entire village, with the entire village. When it came time for my brother's turn, I saw Don Manuel—white as January snow on the mountain, and moving like the surface of the lake when it is stirred by the northeast wind—come up to him with the holy wafer in his hand, which trembled violently as it reached out to Lazarus's mouth; at that moment the priest had an instant of faintness and the wafer dropped to the ground. My brother himself recovered it and placed it in his mouth. The people saw the tears on Don Manuel's face, and everyone wept, saying: "What great love he bears!" And then, because it was dawn, a cock crowed.

On returning home I locked myself in with my brother; alone with him I put my arms around his neck and kissed him.

"Lazarus, Lazarus, what joy you have given us all today; the entire village, the living and the dead, and especially our mother. Did you see how Don Manuel wept for joy? What joy you have given us all!"

"It was for that reason that I did what I did," he answered me.

"For what? To give us pleasure? Surely you did it for your own sake, first of all; because of your conversion."

And then Lazarus, my brother, grown as pale and tremulous as Don Manuel when he was giving Communion, bade me sit down, in the very chair where our mother used to sit. He took a deep breath, and, in the intimate tone of a familiar and domestic confession, he told me:

"Angelita, the time has come when I must tell you the truth, the absolute truth, and I shall tell you because I must, because I cannot, I ought not, conceal it from you, and because, sooner or later, you are bound to intuit it anyway, if only halfway—which would be worse."

Thereupon, serenely and tranquilly, in a subdued voice, he recounted a tale that drowned me in a lake of sorrow. He told how Don Manuel had appealed to him, particularly during the walks to the ruins of the old Cistercian abbey, to set a good example, to avoid scandalizing the townspeople, to take part in the religious life of the community, to feign belief even if he did not feel any, to conceal his own ideas—all this without attempting in any way to catechize him, to instruct him in religion, or to effect a true conversion.

"But is it possible?" I asked in consternation.

"Possible and true. When I said to him: 'Is this you, the priest, who suggests I dissimulate?' he replied, hesitatingly: 'Dissimulate? Not at all! That is not dissimulation. "Dip your fingers in holy water, and you will end by believing," as someone said.' And I, gazing into his eyes, asked him: 'And you, celebrating the Mass, have you ended by believing?' He looked away and stared out at the lake, until his eyes filled with tears. And it was in this way that I came to understand his secret."

"Lazarus!" I cried out, incapable of another word.

At that moment the fool Blasillo came along our street, crying out his: "My God, my God, why hast Thou forsaken me?" And Lazarus shuddered, as if he had heard the voice of Don Manuel, or of Christ.

"It was then," my brother at length continued, "that I really understood his motives and his saintliness; for a saint he is, Sister, a true saint. In trying to convert me to his holy cause—for it is a holy cause, a most holy cause—he was not attempting to score a triumph, but rather was doing it to protect the peace, the happiness, the illusions, perhaps, of his charges. I understood that if he thus deceives them—if it *is* deceit—it is not for his own advantage. I submitted to his logic,—and that was my conversion.

"I shall never forget the day on which I said to him: 'But, Don Manuel, the truth, the truth, above all!'; and he, all a-tremble, whispered in my ear—though we were all alone in the middle of the countryside—'The truth? The truth, Lazarus, is perhaps something so unbearable, so terrible, something so deadly, that simple people could not live with it!'

" 'And why do you show me a glimpse of it now, here, as if we were in the confessional?' I asked. And he said: 'Because if I did not, I would be so tormented by it, so tormented, that I would finally shout it in the middle of the plaza, which I must never, never, never do . . . I am put here to give life to the souls of my charges, to make them happy, to make them dream they are immortal—and not to destroy them. The important thing is that they live sanely, in concord with each other,—and with the truth, with my truth, they could not live at all. Let them live. That is what the Church does, it lets them live. As for true religion, all religions are true as long as they give spiritual life to the people who profess them, as long as they console them for having been born only to die. And for each people the truest religion is their own, the religion that made them . . . And mine? Mine consists in consoling myself by consoling others, even though the consolation I give them is not ever mine.' I shall never forget his words."

"But then this Communion of yours has been a sacrilege," I dared interrupt, regretting my words as soon as I said them.

"Sacrilege? What about the priest who gave it to me? And his Masses?"

"What martyrdom!" I exclaimed.

"And now," said my brother, "there is one more person to console the people."

"To deceive them, you mean?" I said.

"Not at all," he replied, "but rather to confirm them in their faith."

"And they, the people, do they really believe, do you think?"

"About that, I know nothing! . . . They probably believe without trying, from force of habit, tradition. The important thing is not to stir them up. To let them live from their thin sentiments, without acquiring the torments of luxury. Blessed are the poor in spirit!"

"That then is the sentiment you have learned from Don Manuel. . . . And tell me, do you feel you have carried out your promise to our mother on her deathbed, when you promised to pray for her?"

"Do you think I *could* fail her? What do you take me for, sister? Do you think I would go back on my word, my solemn promise made at the hour of death to a mother?"

"I don't know. . . . You might have wanted to deceive her so she could die in peace."

"The fact is, though, that if I had not lived up to my promise, I would be totally miserable."

"And . . ."

"I carried out my promise and I have not neglected for a single day to pray for her."

"Only for her?"

"Well, now, for whom else?"

"For yourself! And now, for Don Manuel."

We parted and went to our separate rooms. I to weep through the night, praying for the conversion of my brother and of Don Manuel. And Lazarus, to what purpose, I know not.

From that day on I was fearful of finding myself alone with Don Manuel, whom I continued to aid in his pious works. And he seemed to sense my inner state and to guess at its cause. When at last I came to him in the confessional's penitential tribunal (who was the judge, and who the offender?) the two of us, he and I, bowed our heads in silence and began to cry. It was he, finally, Don Manuel, who broke the terrible silence, with a voice which seemed to issue from the tomb:

"Angelita, you have the same faith you had when you were ten, don't you? You believe, don't you?"

"I believe, Father."

"Then go on believing. And if doubts come to torment you, suppress them utterly, even to yourself. The main thing is to live . . ."

I summoned up courage, and dared to ask, trembling:

"But, Father, do you believe?"

For a brief moment he hesitated, and then, mastering himself, he said:

"I believe!"

"In what, Father, in what? Do you believe in the after life? Do you believe that in dying we do not die in every way, completely? Do you believe that we will see each other again, that we will love each other in a world to come? Do you believe in another life?"

The poor saint was sobbing.

"My child, leave off, leave off!"

Now, when I come to write this memoir, I ask myself: Why did he not deceive me? Why did he not deceive me as he deceived the others? Why did he afflict himself? Why could he not deceive himself, or why could he not deceive me? And I want to believe that he was afflicted because he could not deceive himself into deceiving me.

"And now," he said, "pray for me, for your brother, and for yourself—for all of us. We must go on living. And giving life."

And, after a pause:

"Angelita, why don't you marry?"

"You know why I do not."

"No, no; you must marry. Lazarus and I will find you a suitor. For it would be good for you to marry, and rid yourself of these obsessions."

"Obsessions, Don Manuel?"

"I know well enough what I am saying. You should not torment yourself for the sake of others, for each of us has more than enough to do answering for himself."

"That it should be you, Don Manuel, who says this! That you should advise me to marry and answer for myself alone and not suffer over others! That it should be you!"

"Yes, you are right, Angelita. I am no longer sure of what I say. I am no longer sure of what I say since I began to confess to you. Only, one must go on living. Yes! One must live!"

And when I rose to leave the church, he asked me:

"Now, Angelita, in the name of the people, do you absolve me?"

I felt pierced by a mysterious and priestly prompting and said:

"In the name of the Father, the Son and the Holy Ghost, I absolve you, Father."

We quitted the church, and as I went out I felt the quickening of maternity within me.

My brother, now totally devoted to the work of Don Manuel, had become his closest and most zealous collaborator and companion. They were bound together, moreover, by their common secret. Lazarus accompanied the priest on his visits to the sick, and to schools, and he placed his resources at the disposition of the saintly man. A little more zeal, and he would have learned to help celebrate Mass. All the while he was sounding deeper in the unfathomable soul of the priest.

"What manliness!" he exclaimed to me once. "Yesterday, as we walked along the lake he said: 'There lies my direst temptation.' When I interrogated him with my eyes, he went on: 'My poor father, who was close to ninety when he died, was tormented all his life, as he confessed to me himself, by a temptation to suicide, by an instinct to self-destruction which had come to him from a time before memory—from birth, from his *nation,* as he said—and was forced to fight against it always. And this fight grew to be his life. So as not to succumb to this temptation he was forced to take precautions, to guard his life. He told me of terrible episodes. His urge was a form of madness,—and I have inherited it. How that water beckons me in its deep quiet! . . . an apparent quietude reflecting the sky like a mirror—and beneath it the hidden current! My life, Lazarus, is a kind of continual suicide, or a struggle against suicide, which is the same thing. . . . Just so long as our people go on living!' And then he added: 'Here the river eddies to form a lake, so that later, flowing down the plateau, it may form into cascades, waterfalls, and torrents, hurling itself through gorges and chasms. Thus does life eddy in the village; and the temptation to suicide is the greater beside the still waters which at night reflect the stars, than it is beside the crashing falls which drive one back in fear. Listen, Lazarus, I have helped poor villagers to die well, ignorant, illiterate villagers, who had scarcely ever been out of their village, and I have learned from their own lips, or divined it when they were silent, the real cause of their sickness unto death, and there at the head of their deathbed I have been able to see into the black abyss of their life-weariness. A weariness a thousand times worse than hunger! For our part, Lazarus, let us go on with our kind of suicide of working for the people, and let them dream their life as the lake dreams the heavens.'

"Another time," said my brother, "as we were coming back, we spied a country girl, a goatherd, standing erect on a height of the mountain slope overlooking the lake and she was singing in a voice fresher than its waters. Don Manuel took hold of me, and pointing to her said: 'Look, it's as though time had stopped, as though this country girl had always been there just as she is, singing in the way she is, and as though she would always be there, as she was before my consciousness began, as she will be when it is past. That girl is a part of nature—not of history—along with the rocks, the clouds, the trees, and the waters.' He has such a subtle feeling for nature, he infuses it with spirit!

"I shall not forget the day when snow was falling and he asked me: 'Have you ever seen a greater mystery, Lazarus, than the snow falling, and dying, in the lake, while a hood is laid upon the mountain?' "

Don Manuel had to moderate and temper my brother's zeal and his neophyte's rawness. As soon as he heard that Lazarus was going about inveighing against some of the popular superstitions he told him forcefully:

"Leave them alone! It's difficult enough making them understand where orthodox belief leaves off and where superstition begins. It's hard enough, especially for us. Leave them alone, then, as long as they get some comfort. . . . It's better for them to believe everything, even things that contradict one another, than to believe nothing. The idea that someone who believes too much ends by not believing in anything is a Protestant notion. Let us not protest! Protestation destroys contentment and peace."

My brother told me, too, about one moonlit night when they were returning to town along the lake (whose surface a mountain breeze was stirring, so that the moonbeams topped the whitecaps), Don Manuel turned to him and said:

"Look, the water is reciting the litany and saying: *ianua caeli, ora pro nobis;* gate of heaven, pray for us."

Two evanescent tears fell from his lashes to the grass, where the light of the full moon shone upon them like dew.

And time went hurrying by, and my brother and I began to notice that Don Manuel's spirits were failing, that he could no longer control completely the deep rooted sadness which consumed him; perhaps some treacherous illness was undermining his body and soul. In an effort to rouse his interest, Lazarus spoke to him of the good effect the organization of a type of Catholic agrarian syndicate would have.

"A syndicate?" Don Manuel repeated sadly. "A syndicate? And what is that? The Church is the only syndicate I know. And you have certainly heard 'My kingdom is not of this world.' Our kingdom, Lazarus, is not of this world . . ."

"And of the other?"

Don Manuel bowed his head:

"The other is here. Two kingdoms exist in this world. Or rather, the other world. . . . Ah, I don't really know what I'm saying. But as for the syndicate, that's a vestige from your days of 'progressivism.' No, Lazarus, no; religion does not exist to resolve the economic or political conflicts of this world, which God handed over to men for their disputes. Let men think and act as they will, let them console themselves for having been born, let them live as happily as possible in the illusion that all this has a purpose. I don't propose to advise the poor to submit to the rich, nor to suggest to the rich that they subordinate themselves to the poor; but rather to preach resignation in everyone, and charity toward everyone. For even the rich man must resign himself—to his riches, and to life; and the poor man must show charity—even to the rich. The Social Question? Ignore it, for it is none of our business. So, a new society is on the way, in which there will be neither rich nor poor, in which wealth will be justly divided, in which everything will belong to everyone—and so, what then? Won't this general well-being and comfort lead to even greater tedium and weariness of life? I know well enough that one of those chiefs of what they call the Social Revolution has already said that religion is the opium of the people. Opium . . . Opium . . . Yes, opium it is. We should give them opium, and help them sleep, and dream. I, myself, with my mad activity, give myself opium. And still I don't manage to sleep well, let alone dream well. . . . What a fearful nightmare! . . . I, too, can say, with the Divine Master: 'My soul is weary unto death.' No, Lazarus, no; no syndicates for us. If *they* organize them, well and good—they would be distracting themselves in that way. Let them play at syndicates, if that makes them happy."

The entire village began to realize that Don Manuel's spirit was weakening, that his strength was waning. His very voice—that miracle of a voice—acquired a kind of quaking. Tears came into his eyes for any reason whatever—or for no reason. Whenever he spoke to people about the other world, about the other life, he was compelled to pause at frequent intervals, and he would close his eyes. "It is a vision," people would say, "he has a vision of what lies ahead." At such moments the fool Blasillo was the first to break into tears. He wept copiously these days, crying now more than he laughed, and even his laughter had the sound of tears.

The last Easter Week which Don Manuel was to celebrate among us, in this world, in this village of ours, arrived, and all the village sensed the impending end of tragedy. And how the words did strike home when for the last time Don Manuel cried out before us: "My God, my God, why hast Thou forsaken me?"! And when he repeated the words of the Lord to the Good Thief ("All thieves are good," Don Manuel used to tell us): "Tomorrow shalt thou be with me in Paradise." . . . ! And then, the last general Communion which our saint was to give! When he came to my brother to give him the

Host—his hand steady this time—, just after the liturgical "... *in vitam aeternam,*" he bent down and whispered to him: "There is no other life but this, no life more eternal ... let them dream it eternal ... let it be eternal for a few years ..."

And when he came to me he said: "Pray, my child, pray for us all." And then, something so extraordinary happened that I carry it now in my heart as the greatest of mysteries: he bent over and said, in a voice which seemed to belong to the other world: "... and pray, too, for our Lord Jesus Christ."

I stood up, going weak as I did so, like a somnambulist. Everything around me seemed dream-like. And I thought: "Am I to pray, too, for the lake and the mountain?" And next: "Am I bewitched, then?" Home at last, I took up the crucifix my mother had held in her hands when she had given up her soul to God, and, gazing at it through my tears and recalling the "My God, my God, why hast Thou forsaken me?" of our two Christs, the one of this earth and the other of this village, I prayed: "Thy will be done on earth as it is in heaven," and then, "And lead us not into temptation. Amen." After this I turned to the statue of the Mater Dolorosa—her heart transfixed by seven swords—which had been my poor mother's most sorrowful comfort, and I prayed again: "Holy Mary, Mother of God, pray for us sinners, now and in the hour of our death. Amen." I had scarcely finished the prayer, when I asked myself: "Sinners? Sinners are we? And what is our sin, what is it?" And all day I brooded over the question.

The next day I presented myself before Don Manuel—Don Manuel now in the full sunset of his magnificent religiosity—and I said to him:

"Do you remember, my Father, years ago when I asked you a certain question you answered: 'That question you must not ask me; for I am ignorant; there are learned doctors of the Holy Mother Church who will know how to answer you'?"

"Do I remember? . . . Of course. And I remember I told you those were questions put to you by the Devil."

"Well, then, Father, I have come again, bedeviled, to ask you another question put to me by my Guardian Devil."

"Ask it."

"Yesterday, when you gave me Communion, you asked me to pray for all of us, and even for . . ."

"That's enough! . . . Go on."

"I arrived home and began to pray; when I came to the part 'Pray for us sinners, now and at the hour of our death,' a voice in me asked:

'Sinners? Sinners are we? And what is our sin?' What is our sin, Father?"

"Our sin?" he replied. "A great doctor of the Spanish Catholic Apostolic Church has already explained it; the great doctor of *Life is a Dream* has written 'The greatest sin of man is to have been born.' That, my child, is our sin; to have been born."

"Can it be atoned, Father?"

"Go and pray again. Pray once more for us sinners, now and at the hour of our death. . . . Yes, at length the dream is atoned . . . at length life is atoned . . . at length the cross of birth is expiated and atoned, and the drama comes to an end. . . . And as Calderón said, to have done good, to have feigned good, even in dreams, is something which is not lost."

The hour of his death arrived at last. The entire village saw it come. And he made it his finest lesson. For he would not die alone or at rest. He died preaching to his people in the church. But first, before being carried to the church (his paralysis made it impossible for him to move), he summoned Lazarus and me to his bedside. Alone there, the three of us together, he said:

"Listen to me: watch over these poor sheep; find some comfort for them in living, and let them believe what I could not. And Lazarus, when your hour comes, die as I die, as Angela will die, in the arms of the Holy Mother Church, Catholic, Apostolic, and Roman; that is to say, of the Holy Mother Church of Valverde de Lucerna. And now, farewell; until we never meet again, for this dream of life is coming to an end . . ."

"Father, Father," I cried out.

"Do not grieve, Angela, only go on praying for all sinners, for all who have been born. Let them dream, let them dream . . . O, what a longing I have to sleep, to sleep, sleep without end, sleep for all eternity, and never dream! Forgetting this dream! . . . When they go to bury me, let it be in a box made from the six planks I cut from the old walnut tree—poor old tree!—in whose shade I played as a child, when I began the dream. . . . In those days, I did really believe in life everlasting. That is to say, it seems to me now that I believed. For a child, to believe is the same as to dream. And for a people, too. . . . You'll find those six planks I cut at the foot of the bed."

He was seized by a sudden fit of choking, and then, composing himself once more, he went on:

"You will recall that when we prayed together, animated by a common sentiment, a community of spirit, and we came to the final verse of the Creed, you will remember that I would fall silent. . . . When the Israelites were coming to the end of their wandering in the desert, the Lord told Aaron and Moses that because they had not believed in Him they would not set foot in the Promised Land with their people; and he bade them climb the heights of Mount Hor, where Moses ordered Aaron stripped of his garments, so that Aaron died there, and then Moses went up from the plains of Moab to Mount Nebo, to the top of Pisgah, looking into Jericho, and the Lord showed him all of the land promised to His people, but said to him: 'You will not go there.' And there Moses died, and no one knew his grave. And he left Joshua to be chief in his place. You, Lazarus, must be my Joshua, and if you can make the sun stand still, make it stop, and never mind progress. Like Moses, I have seen the face of God—our supreme dream—face to face, and as you already know, and as the Scripture says, he who sees God's face, he who sees the eyes of the dream, the eyes with which He looks at us, will die inexorably and forever. And therefore, do not let our people, so long as they live, look into the face of God. Once dead, it will no longer matter, for then they will see nothing . . ."

"Father, Father, Father," I cried again.

And he said:

"Angela, you must pray always, so that all sinners may go on dreaming, until they die, of the resurrection of the flesh and the life everlasting . . ."

I was expecting "and who knows it might be . . ." But instead, Don Manuel had another attack of coughing.

"And now," he finally went on, "and now, in the hour of my death, it is high time to have me brought, in this very chair, to the church, so that I may take leave there of my people, who await me."

He was carried to the church and brought, in his armchair, into the chancel, to the foot of the altar. In his hands he held a crucifix. My brother and I stood close to him, but the fool Blasillo wanted to stand even closer. He wanted to grasp Don Manuel by the hand, so that he could kiss it. When some of the people nearby tried to stop him, Don Manuel rebuked them and said:

"Let him come closer. . . . Come, Blasillo, give me your hand."

The fool cried for joy. And then Don Manuel spoke:

"I have very few words left, my children; I scarcely feel I have strength enough left to die. And then, I have nothing new to tell you, either. I have already said everything I have to say. Live with each other in peace and contentment, in the hope that we will all see each other again some day, in that other Valverde de Lucerna up there among the nighttime stars, the stars which the lake reflects over the image of the reflected mountain. And pray, pray to the Most Blessed Mary, and to our Lord. Be good . . . that is enough. Forgive me whatever wrong I may have done you inadvertently or unknowingly. After I give you my blessing, let us pray together, let us say the Paternoster, the Ave Maria, the Salve, and the Creed."

Then he gave his blessing to the whole village, with the crucifix held in his hand, while the women and children cried and even some of the men wept softly. Almost at once the prayers were begun. Don Manuel listened to them in silence, his hand in the hand of Blasillo the fool, who began to fall asleep to the sound of the praying. First the Paternoster, with its "Thy will be done on earth as it is in heaven"; then the Ave Maria, with its "Pray for us sinners, now and in the hour of our death"; followed by the Salve, with its "mourning and weeping in this vale of tears"; and finally, the Creed. On reaching "The resurrection of the flesh and life everlasting" the people sensed that their saint had yielded up his soul to God. It was not necessary to close his eyes even, for he died with them closed. When an attempt was made to wake Blasillo, it was found that he, too, had fallen asleep in the Lord forever. So that later there were two bodies to be buried.

The village immediately repaired en masse to the house of the saint to carry away holy relics, to divide up pieces of his garments among themselves, to carry off whatever they could find as a memento of the blessed martyr. My brother preserved his breviary, between the pages of which he discovered a carnation, dried as in a herbarium and mounted on a piece of paper, and upon the paper a cross and a certain date.

No one in the village seemed able to believe that Don Manuel was dead; everyone expected to see him—perhaps some of them did—taking his daily walk along the side of the lake, his figure mirrored in the water, or silhouetted against the background of the mountain. They continued to hear his voice, and they all visited his grave, around which a veritable cult sprang up, old women "possessed by devils" came to touch the cross of walnut, made with his own hands from the tree which had yielded the six planks of his casket.

The ones who least of all believed in his death were my brother and I. Lazarus carried on the tradition of the saint, and he began to compile a record of the priest's words. Some of the conversations in this account of mine were made possible by his notes.

"It was he," said my brother, "who made me into a new man. I was a true Lazarus whom he raised from the dead. He gave me faith."

"Ah, faith . . ."

"Yes, faith, faith in the charity of life, in life's joy. It was he who cured me of my delusion of 'progress,' of my belief in its political implications. For there are, Angela, two types of dangerous and harmful men: those who, convinced of life beyond the grave, of the resurrection of the flesh, torment other people—like the inquisitors they are—so that they will despise this life as a transitory thing and work for the other life; and then, there are those who, believing only in this life . . ."

"Like you, perhaps . . ."

"Yes, and like Don Manuel. Believing only in this world, this second group looks forward to some vague future society and exerts every effort to prevent the populace finding consoling joy from belief in another world . . ."

"And so . . ."

"The people should be allowed to live with their illusion."

The poor priest who came to the parish to replace Don Manuel found himself overwhelmed in Valverde de Lucerna by the memory of the saint, and he put himself in the hands of my brother and myself for guidance. He wanted only to follow in the footsteps of the saint. And my brother told him: "Very little theology, Father, very little theology. Religion, religion, religion." Listening to him, I smiled to myself, wondering if this was not a kind of theology, too.

I had by now begun to fear for my poor brother. From the time Don Manuel died it could scarcely be said that he lived. Daily he went to the priest's tomb; for hours on end he stood gazing into the lake. He was filled with nostalgia for deep, abiding peace.

"Don't stare into the lake so much," I begged him.

"Don't worry. It's not this lake which draws me, nor the mountain. Only, I cannot live without his help."

"And the joy of living, Lazarus, what about the joy of living?"

"That's for others. Not for those of us who have seen God's face, those of us on whom the Dream of Life has gazed with His eyes."

"What; are you preparing to go and see Don Manuel?"

"No, sister, no. Here at home now, between the two of us, the whole truth—bitter as it may be, bitter as the sea into which the sweet waters of our lake flow—the whole truth for you, who are so set against it . . ."

"No, no, Lazarus. You are wrong. Your truth is not the truth."

"It's my truth."

"Yours, perhaps, but surely not . . ."

"His, too."

"No, Lazarus. Not now, it isn't. Now, he must believe otherwise; now he must believe . . ."

"Listen, Angela, once Don Manuel told me that there are truths which, though one reveals them to oneself, must be kept from others; and I told him that telling me was the same as telling himself. And then he said, he confessed to me, that he thought that more than one of the great saints, perhaps the very greatest himself, had died without believing in the other life."

"Is it possible?"

"All too possible! And now, sister, you must be careful that here, among the people, no one even suspects our secret . . ."

"Suspect it?" I cried in amazement. "Why even if I were to try, in a fit of madness, to explain it to them, they wouldn't understand it. The people do not understand your words, they understand your actions much better. To try and explain all this to them would be like reading some pages from Saint Thomas Aquinas to eight-year-old children, in Latin."

"All the better. In any case, when I am gone, pray for me and for him and for all of us."

At length, his own time came. A sickness which had been eating away at his robust nature seemed to flare with the death of Don Manuel.

"I don't so much mind dying," he said to me in his last days, "as the fact that with me another piece of Don Manuel dies too. The remainder of him must live on with you. Until, one day, even we dead will die forever."

When he lay in the throes of death, the people of the village came in to bid him farewell (as is customary in our towns) and they commended his soul to the care of Don Manuel Bueno, Martyr. My brother said nothing to them; he had nothing more to say. He had already said everything there was to say. He had become a link between the two Valverde de Lucernas—the one at the bottom of the lake and the one reflected in its surface. He was already one more of us who had died of life, and, in his way, one more of our saints.

I was desolate, more than desolate; but I was, at least, among my own people, in my own village. Now, having lost my San Manuel, the father of my soul, and my own Lazarus, my more than carnal brother, my spiritual brother, now it is I realize that I have aged. But, have I really lost them then? Have I grown old? Is my death approaching?

I must live! And he taught me to live, he taught us to live, to feel life, to feel the meaning of life, to merge with the soul of the mountain, with the soul of the lake, with the soul of the village, to lose ourselves in them so as to remain in them forever. He taught me by his life to lose myself in the life of the people of my village, and I no longer felt the passing of the hours, and the days, and the years, any more than I felt the passage of the water in the lake. It began to seem that my life would always be thus. I no longer felt myself growing old. I no longer lived in myself, but in my people, and my people lived in me. I tried to speak as they spoke, as they spoke without trying. I went into the street—it was the one highway—and, since I knew everyone, I lived in them and forgot myself (while, on the other hand, in Madrid, where I went once with my brother, I had felt a terrible loneliness, since I knew no one, and had been tortured by the sight of so many unknown people).

Now, as I write this memoir, this confession of my experience with saintliness, with a saint, I am of the opinion that Don Manuel Bueno, my Don Manuel, and my brother, too, died believing they did not believe, but that, without believing in their belief, they actually believed, with resignation and in desolation.

But why, I have asked myself repeatedly, did not Don Manuel attempt to convert my brother deceitfully, with a lie, pretending to be a believer himself without being one? And I have finally come to think that Don Manuel realized he would not be able to delude him, that with him a fraud would not do, that only through the truth, with his truth, would he be able to convert him; that he knew he would accomplish nothing if he attempted to enact the comedy—the tragedy, rather—which he played out for the benefit of the people. And thus did he win him over, in effect, to his pious fraud; thus did he win him over to the cause of life with the truth of death. And thus did he win me, who never permitted anyone to see through his divine, his most saintly, game. For I believed then, and I believe now, that God—as part of I know not what sacred and inscrutable purpose—caused them to believe they were unbelievers. And that at the moment of their passing, perhaps, the blindfold was removed.

And I, do I believe?

As I write this—here in my mother's old house, and I past my fiftieth year and my memories growing as dim and blanched as my hair—outside it is snowing, snowing upon the lake, snowing upon the mountain, upon the memory of my father, the stranger, upon the memory of my mother, my brother Lazarus, my people, upon the memory of my San Manuel, and even on the memory of the poor fool Blasillo, my Saint Blasillo—and may he help me in heaven! The snow effaces corners and blots out shadows, for even in the night it shines and illuminates. Truly, I do not know what is true and what is false, nor what I saw and what I merely dreamt—or rather, what I dreamt and what I merely saw—, nor what I really knew or what I merely believed true. Neither do I know whether or not I am transferring to this paper, white as the snow outside, my consciousness, for it to remain in writing, leaving me without it. But why, any longer, cling to it?

Do I really understand any of it? Do I really believe in any of it? Did what I am writing about here actually take place, and did it take place in just the way I tell it? Is it possible for such things to happen? Is it possible that all this is more than a dream dreamed within another dream? Can it be that I, Angela Carballino, a woman in her fifties, am the only one in this village to be assailed by far-fetched thoughts, thoughts unknown to everyone else? And the others, those around me, do they believe? And what does it mean, to believe? At least they go on living. And now they believe in San Manuel Bueno, Martyr, who, with no hope of immortality for himself, preserved their hope in it.

It appears that our most illustrious bishop, who set in motion the process for beatifying our saint from Valverde de Lucerna, is intent on writing an account of Don Manuel's life, something which would serve as a guide for the perfect parish priest, and with this end in mind he is gathering information of every sort. He has repeatedly solicited information from me; more than once he has come to see me; and I have supplied him with all sorts of facts. But I have never revealed the tragic secret of Don Manuel and my brother. And it is curious that he has never suspected. I trust that what I have set down here will never come to his knowledge. For, all temporal authorities are to be avoided; I fear all authorities on this earth—even when they are church authorities.

But this is an end to it. Let its fate be what it will . . .

How, you ask, did this document, this memoir of Angela Carballino fall into my hands? That, reader, is something I must keep secret. I have transcribed it for you just as it is written, just as it came to me, with only a few, a very few editorial emendations. It recalls to you other things I have written? This fact does not gainsay its objectivity, its originality. Moreover, for all I know, perhaps I created real, actual beings, independent of me, beyond my control, characters with immortal souls. For all I know, Augusto Perez in my novel *Mist*[2] was right when he claimed to be more real, more objective than I myself, who had thought to have invented him. As for the reality of this San Manuel Bueno, Martyr—as he is revealed to me by his disciple and spiritual daughter Angela Carballino—of his reality it has not occurred to me to doubt. I believe in it more than the saint himself did. I believe in it more than I do in my own reality.

And now, before I bring this epilogue to a close, I wish to recall to your mind, patient reader, the ninth verse of the Epistle of the forgotten Apostle, Saint Judas—what power in a name!—where we are told how my heavenly patron, St. Michael Archangel (Michael means

2. In the denouement of *Mist,* the protagonist Augusto Perez turns on Unamuno, and tells him that he, a creation of human thought and genius, is more real than his author, a product of blind animality.

"Who such as God?" and archangel means archmessenger) disputed with the Devil (Devil means accuser, prosecutor) over the body of Moses, and would not allow him to carry it off as a prize, to damnation. Instead, he told the Devil: "May the Lord rebuke thee." And may he who wishes to understand, understand!

I would like also, since Angela Carballino injected her own feelings into her narrative—I don't know how it could have been otherwise—to comment on her statement to the effect that if Don Manuel and his disciple Lazarus had confessed their convictions to the people, they, the people, would not have understood. Nor, I should like to add, would they have believed the pair. They would have believed in their works and not their words. And works stand by themselves, and need no words to back them up. In a village like Valverde de Lucerna one makes one's confession by one's conduct.

And as for faith, the people scarce know what it is, and care less.

I am well aware of the fact that no action takes place in this narrative, this *novelistic* narrative, if you will—the novel is, after all, the most intimate, the truest history, so that I scarcely understand why some people are outraged to have the Bible called a novel, when such a designation actually sets it above some mere chronicle or other. In short, nothing happens. But I hope that this is because everything that takes place happens, and, instead of coming to pass, and passing away, remains forever, like the lakes and the mountains and the blessed simple souls fixed firmly beyond faith and despair, the blessed souls who, in the lakes and the mountains, outside history, in their divine novel, take refuge.

SALAMANCA, 1930

Gateway Editions

ANSKY, S., *The Dybbuk*
AQUINAS, ST. THOMAS, *An Introduction to Metaphysics*
AQUINAS, ST. THOMAS, *Treatise on Law*
AUGUSTINE, ST., *Enchiridion of Faith, Hope and Love*
AUGUSTINE, ST., *The Political Writings*
BIERCE, AMBROSE, *Ambrose Bierce's Civil War*
BOETHIUS, *The Consolation of Philosophy*
BUCKLEY, WILLIAM F., JR., *God and Man at Yale*
BURKE, EDMUND, *Selected Writings*
BURNHAM, JAMES, *The Machiavellians*
BURNHAM, JAMES, *Suicide of the West*
CHAMBERS, WHITTAKER, *Odyssey of a Friend*
CHAMBERS, WHITTKAER, *Witness*
CLAUSEEWITZ, KARL von, *War, Politics, and Power*
CROSSMAN, RICHARD H., *God That Failed*
CUSTINE, MARQUIS de, *Journey for Our Time*
FREUD, SIGMUND, *Origin and Development of Psychoanalysis*
GUARDINI, ROMANO, *The Lord*
HEIDEGGER, MARTIN, *Existence and Being*
HITTI, PHILIP K., *The Arabs: A Short History*
HITTI, PHILIP K., *Islam: A Way of Life*
JAKI, STANLEY, *Brain, Mind, and Computers*
JAKI STANLEY, *God and the Cosmologists*
JAKI, STANLEY, *The Purpose of It All*
JAKI, STANLEY, *The Savior of Science*
KIRK, RUSSELL, *The Conservative Mind*
LOCKE, JOHN, *Reasonableness of Christianity*
MARX, KARL, *Communist Manifesto*
MARX, KARL, *Das Kapital*
MASTROBUONO, ANTONIO C., *Dante's Journey of Sanctification*
MENCKEN, H. L., *H. L. Mencken's Smart Set Criticism*
NIETZSCHE, FRIEDRICH, *Beyond Good and Evil*
NIETZSCHE, FRIEDRICH, *Philosophy in the Tragic Age of the Greeks*
PICARD, MAX, *Flight from God*
PICARD, MAX, *World of Silence*
PICO della MIRANDOLA, GIOVANNI, *Oration on the Dignity of Man*
PLATO, *Euthyphro, Crito, Apology, and Symposium*
RYN, CLAES, *Will, Imagination and Reason*
SARTRE, JEAN-PAUL, *Existential Psychoanalysis*
SOLZHENITSYN, ALEXANDER, *From Under the Rubble*
SOSEKI, NATSUME, *Kokoro*
SOSEKI, NATSUME, *Three Cornered World*
STEVENSON, ROBERT LOUIS, *Selected Essays*
UNAMUNO, MIGUEL de, *Abel Sanchez*
VOEGELIN, ERIC, *Science, Politics and Gnosticism*
MISES, LUDWIG von, *Economic Policy*